"You are a pain in the neck, Wynn."

Zack briefly kissed her, then continued. "I've never met a woman who wanted a man, yet insulted his manhood with every other breath."

Wynn's gaze skipped down his body to his lap, her toes curling inside her gym shoes.

"One of these days," he added while licking her ear and driving her insane, "I'm going to prove it to you."

"How?" She had no idea what he wanted to prove, but whatever it might be, she was all for it.

"Will you be at your hammock tonight?"

Hope and excitement flared inside her. "Yes. Sure, of course."

Seeing her expression, he warned, "Wynn, I'm not making any promises about anything. If we meet tonight, it's strictly for sex."

Her hopes plummeted, but the excitement was still there. On the one hand, she'd never been a woman for casual sex. But on the other, she'd never wanted a man like she wanted Zack....

Dear Reader,

When single dad and sexy paramedic, Zack Grange, first appeared in *Caught in the Act* (Harlequin single title, 0-373-83469-1) we saw how controlled and levelheaded he appeared to be.

Ha! In no time at all, Wynn Lane, an amazon of a woman who exemplifies everything Zack frowns upon, manages to shake him right off his respectable foundation. Wynn moves in next door to Zack and his world will never be the same. Problem is, Zack never knows if he wants to laugh, shout or make love to her.

Rarely have I had so much fun writing a book! I laughed to myself as I constructed various scenes, and I hope you'll do a little laughing, too.

Be sure to check back next month for Josh Marshall's story, *Mr. November,* (Harlequin Temptation #856), and happy reading, everyone!

Lori Foster

Lori Foster
TREAT HER RIGHT

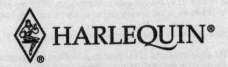

HARLEQUIN®

TORONTO • NEW YORK • LONDON
AMSTERDAM • PARIS • SYDNEY • HAMBURG
STOCKHOLM • ATHENS • TOKYO • MILAN • MADRID
PRAGUE • WARSAW • BUDAPEST • AUCKLAND

To Morgan Arce, this one's for you!
Not only did I enjoy our chats on the phone,
but all the information you shared made the
research on this book a lot of fun!
Thank you so much.

ISBN 0-373-25952-2

TREAT HER RIGHT

Copyright © 2001 by Lori Foster.

Visit us at www.eHarlequin.com

Printed in U.S.A.

1

Zack

"DAMN YOU, CONAN! THAT'S IT!"

Zack Grange jerked upright in his bed, heart pounding, muscles coiled. His sleep-fogged brain felt in a jumble. He'd been dreaming, a very hot dream about a sexy lady—faceless, but with a gorgeous body—and then he'd heard the loud female shout. Caught between drugging sleep and abrupt wakefulness, confusion swamped him.

He looked around his shadowed bedroom and found it as empty as ever. No one lurked in the corners, certainly not the lady he'd been dreaming of, yet the voice had seemed to be right upon him. Heart still tripping, he strained to hear, and caught male laughter floating in through his open window. He frowned.

A glance at the clock showed it to be only seven-thirty. He'd barely been in bed at all, not long enough to recoup from the strenuous night. Certainly not long enough to finish that tempting, now elusive dream.

The deep female voice came again.

"It's not funny, you moron, and you know it," the woman groused, showing no consideration for those people still trying sleep. "I can't believe you did this to me."

"Better you than me, sweetheart." Then, "Ouch! Now that hurt."

Zack threw off his sheet. Wearing only his boxers, he went to the window to look out. He shivered as the morning air washed over his mostly bare body. The mid-September nights were getting cool, but he preferred the fresh air for sleeping. He stretched out aching muscles, still cramped from all the lifting he'd done just a few hours ago, scratched his chest, then slid aside a thin drape and peered down into the yard behind his house.

His was a larger, more private corner lot, and the street behind him ran perpendicular to his own. His bedroom window, at the back of his house, faced the side lot, so that he could see both the front and backyard of the home behind him.

New neighbors, he thought with disgust, noticing the For Sale sign now lying flat, and cardboard boxes piled everywhere around the yard. Squinting against the blinding red haze of a half-risen sun, his tired eyes gritty, he searched for the source of the screeching.

When his gaze finally landed on her, he stared in stunned disbelief.

Extremely curly brown hair was only halfheartedly contained in a sloppy ponytail. He couldn't see the details of her upper body beneath an overlarge, misshapen sweatshirt, but her shorts showed off mile-long, athletic legs and dirty white tennis shoes. Zack surveyed her top to bottom, and because a lot of distance stretched between those two points, it took a good minute.

As a basic male, he immediately considered those long strong legs. With the erotic dream still dancing around the corners of his mind, he pictured them twined around him, or perhaps even over his shoulders, and speculated on how tightly they might hold a man when he was between them, buried deep inside her.

As a discriminating man, he wondered why her hair looked such a wreck and what her upper body might present once out of that awful sweatshirt.

And lastly, as a neighbor, he wanted to groan at the lack of consideration that kept her squawking and carping in a voice too deep and too loud to be called even remotely feminine. The future didn't bode well, not with her living behind him.

"Daddy?"

Zack turned with a smile, but he felt ready to commit murder. Evidently, the noise had awakened his daughter, which meant there would be no going back to bed for him. Exhaustion wrought a groan in protest, but he held out a hand, smiling gently. "Come here, sweetheart. It looks like our new neighbors are moving in."

Rubbing her eyes with a small fist, Dani padded toward him, dragging her favorite fuzzy yellow blanket behind her. Her wee bare feet peeked out from the hem of her nightgown. Standing out around her head, her typically mussed blond hair formed a halo, and one round cheek was creased from her pillow. She reached him and held up her skinny arms. "Let me see," she demanded in her adorable childish voice.

Obligingly, Zack lifted her. His daughter was such a tiny person, even though she was now four. Petite, as her mother had been, he thought, and hugged her close to his naked chest. He breathed in her little girl smell, rubbed his rough cheek against her downy soft hair, kissed her ear.

She liked to be held, and he loved holding her.

As usual, Dani immediately gave him a wet good-morning kiss on his whiskered cheek. She wrapped her arms around his throat, her legs around his waist, and looked out the window. Her blanket caught between them.

Zack waited for her reaction. Dani never failed to amuse him. For a four-year-old, she was very astute, honest to a fault, and he loved her more than life itself.

Most of the kids her age asked constant questions, but not Dani. She made statements instead. Other than two days a week at a preschool, she was always in the company of his friends. Zack assumed her exposure to adults accounted for her speech habits.

"I see her butt," she said with an exaggerated frown.

Startled, Zack lowered his head to peer out the window again, and sure enough, the woman bent at the waist, her legs straight and braced apart for leverage as she tugged on a large box. Her shorts were riding rather high and he could just see the twin moons of her bottom cheeks.

Nice ass, he thought appreciatively, lifting one brow and looking a little harder. Dani poked him, and he shook his head, remembering that this woman had just awakened him from a much-needed sleep and a pleasantly carnal dream. "Wait until she stands up, Dani."

The woman tugged and pulled and when the box broke apart, she fell backward, landing on that nice behind. From somewhere on her porch, a man hooted with loud laughter and called out, "Want some help?"

Zack fancied he could see some of her curly brown hair standing on end. She all but vibrated with temper, then snarled in a voice reminiscent of an enraged cat, "*Go away,* Conan!"

"But I thought you wanted my help?" came the innocent, taunting reply.

"You," she said back, standing up and dusting herself off with enough force to leave bruises on a less hearty woman, "have done enough."

Zack tried to see the mysterious Conan, but couldn't. Her husband? A boyfriend? What kind of name was Conan anyway?

As the woman gained her feet, Dani said in awe, "She's a giant!"

Chuckling, Zack squeezed her. "She looks as tall as me, doesn't she, honey?"

His daughter nodded, watching the woman unload the box with jerky, angry movements, rather than try to move it again. Dani laid her head on Zack's chest, quietly thinking in that way she sometimes did. Zack rubbed her back, waiting to see what she'd say next.

She shocked him speechless by suddenly leaning forward—leaving it up to him to balance her off-balance weight—and cupping her hand to her mouth, she shouted out the window, "Hello!"

The woman turned, looked up with a hand shading her eyes, searching. She spotted them and her frown was replaced by a bright toothy smile. She waved with as much enthusiasm as she'd used to dust her bottom. "Hello there!"

In his underwear, Zack quickly ducked behind the curtain. "*Dani*," he said, ready to muzzle his daughter. "What are you doing?"

She wrinkled her little nose at him. "Jus' being neighborly, like you said I should."

"That was to the old neighbors. We don't even know these people yet."

She wiggled to get down, and when he set her on her feet, she said, "We'll go meet 'em now."

Zack caught her by the back of her cotton nightgown as she started to barrel out of the room. "Hold on, little lady. We have breakfast and chores and washing up to do first, right?"

Again, she wrinkled her nose. "Later."

He almost grinned at her small, sweet hopeful voice—a voice she only used when trying to wrap him around her itty-bitty finger. "Now."

Disgruntled and grumbling under her breath, she trod back to the window and yelled, "I'll be out later!"

The woman laughed. It was a nice rich husky sound,

much better than her screaming. "I'll surely still be here."

Zack looked out, feeling as if he'd landed in the twilight zone. Now that his daughter had drawn attention to them—and the neighbors knew they'd been watched—he couldn't very well ignore them.

The man from the porch sauntered into the yard, smiling. Zack blinked with yet another surprise. Massive, was the only word for him. Built like a large bulldog, he stood a few inches shorter than the woman, but was twice as thick and all muscle. He lifted an arm as stout as a tree trunk and waved.

"I'm Conan Lane," he called out, "and this squawking shrew is Wynonna."

To Zack's amazement and Dani's delight, the woman elbowed Conan hard, making him bend double and wheeze, then she corrected sweetly, "Call me Wynn."

Seeing no hope for it, Zack shouted back, "Zack Grange, and my daughter, Dani."

"Nice to meet you both!" And then to further exasperate him, Wynn said, "Since we're all awake and it's such a beautiful morning, I'll bring over some coffee so we can get acquainted."

Zack stammered, unsure how to deny that audacious imposition, but she'd already turned and hurried into her house, the enormous Conan following her. He frowned down at Dani, who shrugged, grinned, and said, "We better get dressed." And off she dashed, her blanket dragging behind her.

Zack dropped to the side of his bed and scrubbed his

hands over his face. He was badly in need of a shave and a long shower. At the moment he had no doubt his eyes were more red than blue. He'd worked twelve grueling hours last night, tended two especially trying emergencies, and he was starved as well as fatigued.

Luckily, this was his day off, which he'd intended to spend shopping with Dani. Because his daughter liked to play hard, and paid no mind at all to the knees of her jeans or the elbows of her shirts, she was desperately in need of new fall clothes.

He did not want to be bothered with outrageous neighbors.

Especially not neighbors who'd awakened him too early and were too damn large. And loud.

Shoving himself off the bed, he determined to get through the next few minutes with as much politeness and forbearance as he could muster.

The doorbell rang not three minutes later. He'd barely had time to pull on jeans and a sweatshirt. He picked up his running shoes, carrying them loosely in his hand. On his way to the door, he peeked in at Dani. She stood there in a T-shirt and blue-flowered panties, surveying her closet with a studious frown.

Zack leaned on her doorframe. "Dress warm, honey."

She nodded, frowned some more, and looked through her clothes. Zack bit back a grin and asked, "Hard decision?"

She was so intent on her choice, she didn't answer.

Because jeans were a given, he said, "How about a

sweater?'' preferring that over what she might have chosen otherwise—a ratty sweatshirt. He posed it as a suggestion, rather than an instruction, because he knew she liked to make her own decisions—about every-thing—any time he gave her that option.

She nodded agreement. "Okay. What sweater?"

He walked into the room, reached into her closet and pulled out a soft red sweater with multicolored buttons. "This one is nice," he suggested, trying his best to sound serious and sincere.

She studied the sweater, considering, until the door-bell rang again. Snatching it out of his hand, she pushed at him and said, "Go! Go get the door, Dad!"

Zack laughed as he walked away. His daughter, the social butterfly. Most times, Dani didn't give two cents for how she dressed. She'd pull on the same clothes from the night before if Zack didn't get them out of her room and into the hamper fast enough. But let them have company and she agonized. Not that she wanted to wear dresses. Heaven forbid! And anything other than sneakers or boots repulsed her four-year-old sen-sibilities.

But she did like color. Lots and lots of color. Often if left to her own devices, she'd clash so horribly it'd make his eyes glaze.

Still sporting a grin, Zack bounded down the stairs and went to the front door. He turned the locks and opened it, wishing he didn't have to do this today. He'd wanted nothing more than to sleep in, then take a long leisurely soak in the hot tub, eat an enormous breakfast, and spend the day with his daughter.

Now he had to be neighborly.

The second the door opened, the woman looked at him and her smile faded. "Oh dear," she said. "We woke you up, didn't we?"

Zack went mute and stared.

Up close, she seemed even taller, and she did indeed look him in the eye. At six feet tall, that didn't happen to him often. His two best friends, Mick and Josh, were both taller, Mick especially, who stood six foot three. But then they were both guys. They were *not* female.

A light breeze ruffled her flyaway hair, which seemed to have been permanently crimped. The color was nice, a soft honey-brown, lighter around her face where the sun had kissed it. Curls sprung out here and there and everywhere, like miniature springs. He doubted such unruly hair could ever be fully contained.

A soft flush colored her skin—high across her cheekbones, over the bridge of her narrow nose and the tip of her chin—either by the warmth of the day, her exertions, or the bright sunshine. Zack suspected the latter.

Sporting a crooked smile, she stared right back at him with the most unusual hazel eyes he'd ever seen. So light they were almost the color of topaz, they were fringed by thick, impossibly dark lashes, especially given the color of her hair. After a silent moment, her arched brows lifted and her smile stretched into a full-fledged grin.

Zack caught himself. Good God, he'd been staring at

her as if he'd never seen a woman before. He'd been staring at her...*with interest.* He shook his head. "What gave me away?"

"What's that?" She now appeared confused.

"How could you tell that you woke me?"

"Ah. The hair standing on end? The all-night whiskers? Or it could be the bloodshot eyes." She made a tsking sound. "Have you slept at all?"

He ran a hand through his hair and mumbled, "I worked pretty late last night," and left it at that. He wasn't with it enough yet to start rehashing the past evening's events. He pushed the screen door open and stepped aside. "Come on in."

She looked behind her. "Conan will be right along. He's getting some muffins out of the oven. He's a terrific cook."

Conan-the-massive cooked?

The woman held up a carafe. "Fresh coffee. French vanilla. I hope that's okay?"

He hated flavored coffees. "It's fine," he lied, "but totally unnecessary."

"It's the very least I can do now that I know I got you out of bed."

If she hadn't, he thought, perhaps he'd have finished that sexy dream and not been so edgy now. But as it was, he couldn't quite seem to get himself together.

She hesitated at the door. "I really am so sorry. This is my first house and I'm equally stressed and excited and when I get that way, I unfortunately get—" She shrugged in apology. "—loud."

Her honesty was both unexpected and appealing. Zack forced a smile. "I understand."

Yet, she still held back. "I don't mean to barge in. If you have some cups, we could sit here on your porch. We'll share one cup of coffee, chat a little, and that's all, I promise. It's a beautiful morning and we are all awake now, right?"

Great. If he kept her and her husband outside, he could probably get rid of them quicker. "Good idea. Have a seat and I'll go get some cups."

Just then, Dani came dashing down the steps. Zack turned, saw her small feet flying, and said softly but sternly, "Slow down."

She skidded to a halt on the second to the bottom step, gave him a quick, offhand, "Sorry," and looked up at the woman as she finished approaching. "Hi."

Wynn's face lit up with her smile, making those golden eyes glow and the color in her cheeks intensify. "Hello there!" Kneeling down in the doorway, she said, "It's so good to meet you." She held out a hand that Dani took with formality. Zack watched in awe. "I hadn't realized I'd have another female for a neighbor. The Realtor only told me that a single man lived here."

"I'm Dani. My mom died," Dani said, "so it's jus' me and Dad."

Given half a chance, Dani would voice anything that came into her mind. Normally he didn't mind, but this time it rankled.

Her sweater was hiked up in the back and the left leg of her jeans had caught on a cotton sock. Zack smoothed the sweater, tugged the jeans into place, and frowned at her hair. His daughter, bless her heart, had the most impossible baby-fine, flyaway blond hair.

Then he glanced at Wynn again and revised his opinion. Dani had difficult hair, but definitely not the worst.

Softly, probably because she realized Dani had touched on a private topic, Wynn said, "Well, I'm very glad to have you for a neighbor, Dani." She glanced up at Zack warily. "And your dad, too, of course."

Zack took his daughter's hand, not about to leave her alone with a virtual stranger, and said, "Wynn, if you'd like to make yourself comfortable, we'll get the mugs and be right out."

Wynn stood again, stretching out that long tall body. Zack's gaze automatically dropped to her legs, but he quickly pulled it back to her face even as a wave of heat snaked through him. She was married, he thought guiltily, and he had no intention of ogling a neighbor anyway.

Rather than looking put out by his quick, intimate perusal, Wynn smiled. "Sounds good," she murmured, her eyes warm. She turned back to the porch, giving Zack a back view of those strong shapely legs and tight bottom, and the screen door fell shut behind her.

Dani stared up at him, but he shook his head, indicating she should be quiet for a moment. When they reached the kitchen, he plunked her onto a chair opposite him and took a moment to pull on his shoes. That accomplished, he looked at his daughter. "Juice?"

"Apple." Dani swung her feet, then tilted her head. "She's not taller than you."

"No, not quite," Zack said, locating a tray beneath the sink and loading it with three mugs, a glass of apple juice and a bowl of cereal for Dani. "It's close, though. She looked me right in the eye, but she had on thick-soled shoes and I was still barefoot."

Dani squirmed. "I want my hair in a ponytail like hers."

He smiled. Maybe a female neighbor, even a very big one with corkscrew hair, wouldn't be a bad thing. Eloise, Dani's sitter during Zack's working hours, was a very kind, gentle and attentive woman. But she was old enough to be Zack's grandmother, with bluish hair and support hose—not a woman to inspire a young girl.

Zack's company was mostly limited to Mick and Josh, and though Josh knew everything there was to know about legal-aged females, he knew next to nothing about four-year-olds. Since Mick had married, Dani got to visit with Delilah now and then, and the two of them had really hit it off, which proved to Zack that Dani needed a woman around more often.

For Dani's sake, he'd decided he needed a wife. But finding someone appropriate was proving to be more difficult than he'd thought, mostly because he had so little time to look.

When he did have time, he didn't run across any suitable women. A wife would need to be domestic, neat, lovable, and she'd have to understand that his daughter came first. Period.

"A ponytail it is," Zack said, forcing his mind away from that problem. He stroked his big rough fingers through Dani's fine hair. "Why don't you go get your brush and a band, and then come out to the porch?"

"Okay." She slid off the chair and ran from the room again. His daughter never walked when she could run. She was never quiet when she could talk or laugh, and she always fought naps right up until she ran out of gas and all but collapsed. She exuded constant energy, and she had an imagination that often left him floored.

She was his life.

Wynn and Conan were arguing again when Zack opened the screen door. He stalled, uncertain what to do as Wynn poked the bulky bruiser in the chest and threatened his life.

Ignoring most of her diatribe, Conan said, "Ha!" then flicked her earlobe, hard.

Zack's mouth fell open, seeing the physical byplay.

Before he could say anything, Wynn lit up like a live wire, clutching at her ear. "That *hurt!*"

"Well so does your pointy little finger trying to bore holes in my chest."

"Bull." She leaned in to him, nose to nose, and deliberately gave him another, harder prod. "You can't feel anything through that layer of rock and you know it."

Conan rubbed his chest, opened his mouth to say God-only-knew-what, then noticed Zack. He scowled. "You're making a spectacle of yourself in front of your neighbors, Wynonna."

Frozen half in, half out of the door, Zack just stared.

Domestic troubles? God, he didn't want to be involved in this.

Wynn rushed forward and took the tray from him. "Just ignore Conan," she said, "he's a bully."

Conan ran both hands through his blond hair, which Zack noticed wasn't the least bit frizzy, and growled. His eyes turned red and his face blue. "Wynonna, I swear I'm gonna—"

He reached for her and Zack, without really thinking, stepped between them. The tray in Wynn's arms wobbled, but she maintained her grip.

"Look," Zack said, not sure if the woman would need any help or not, "this is none of my business, but—"

Wynn rudely pushed her way around him. "You're gonna what?" she taunted Conan. "What else can you do?"

Conan reached for her again, and Zack grabbed him. *"That's enough,"* he roared.

Zack hadn't had enough sleep, he was still disturbed by the calls he'd made the night before, and he had no tolerance for petty bickering.

And he absolutely, positively, would not put up with a man hurting a woman, not even a pesky too-big neighbor woman he barely knew and who looked like she could damn well defend herself.

Silence fell. Conan, with one brow raised, stared at Zack's hand wrapped around his thick wrist. Zack had big hands, but still, his fingers barely touched.

Conan's gaze shifted to Wynn, and he made a wry face. "A gallant in the making?"

Wynn set the tray down and rushed to put herself between the two men, facing Zack. Her fingers spread wide on his chest, pressing, restraining although he could have easily moved her aside and they both knew it. Wedged between the two of them, she was so close to Zack he felt her breath and the heat of her body. He twitched.

Wynn stared into his face with an expression bordering on wonder, patted him, and then said with quiet sincerity, "Thank you, but Conan would never hurt me, Zack. I promise. He just likes to needle."

Conan, still caught in Zack's unrelenting grasp, snorted at that. But he replied easily, "She's right, you know. I might want to swat her every now and again, but I wouldn't hurt her."

Swat her? Zack peered into Wynn's large golden eyes and imagined all kinds of kinky sexual play between the two of them.

He wasn't sure if he was disgusted or intrigued, and his indecision on the matter was unacceptable. He frowned, feeling very put upon.

Then Conan continued lazily. "Wynn, however, has never shown any such consideration. She's been kicking my ass since we were both in diapers."

Wynn gave Zack an apologetic nod. "It's true. Conan is such a big lug, he's always let me practice up on him."

Conan tugged on his hand, and Zack, feeling numb and rather foolish, and for some damn reason, relieved, released him.

Brother and sister?

"She's so big," Conan continued, "she's always looked older than her age. When she was in ninth grade, college guys were hitting on her! She needed to know how to fight off the cretins. So I've been her personal punching bag for longer than I care to remember."

Still with her hands pressed to Zack's chest, Wynn glanced over her shoulder and smiled. "Not that he feels it," she said to her brother, "regardless of how he carries on." Facing Zack again, she explained, "A steamroller could go over Conan and he's so thick with muscle he wouldn't notice."

Zack inhaled and breathed in the scents of vanilla coffee, fresh blueberry muffins, early morning dew on green grass—and Wynn. She smelled...different. Not sweet. Not exactly spicy. It was more a fresh scent, like a cool fall breeze or the forerunner to a storm. His muscles twitched again.

Damn, but this day was not going at all as planned.

And he could only blame one very big, and somehow very appealing, woman. A woman who was not only his neighbor, but still touching him, still looking at him with a mixture of tenderness, humor, and...hunger.

He'd known tall women, hell, Mick's wife Delilah was tall. But he'd never known such a...*sturdy* woman. Her open hands on his chest were nearly as large as his own. Her shoulders were broad, her bones long. Unlike Delilah, Wynn wasn't delicate.

But she was sexy.

He needed some sleep to be able to deal with the likes of her. And he needed more time.

And most of all, he needed sex, because he knew when he started getting turned on by a loud, pushy amazon, it had been far, far too long.

2

GATHERING HIS scattered wits, Zack looked at both Wynn and Conan, then stepped out of Wynn's reach. "I see," he said, for lack of anything better. His brain was all but empty of responses. This had not been a memorable morning.

Wynn fought off a smile, at his expense. "I do appreciate your consideration for my welfare, though."

The way she said it made him feel ten times more foolish. He could see why Conan thought she needed a good swat. At the moment, he wasn't totally averse to the idea himself.

Conan saved the awkward moment by pouring the coffee. The rich aroma of vanilla intensified, but Zack could still smell *her*. She'd been working and her skin was hot, dewy with her exertions.

He growled low in his throat, hating his basic response to her.

Thankfully unaware of the source of his disgruntlement, Conan said, "Sit down, Zack. You look like we've wrung you out already. And I have to tell you, it's only going to get worse."

How in the hell can it get worse? Zack accepted the coffee and seated himself in a padded chair. Conan sat across from him, Wynn on the settee. Mustering a tone of bland inquiry, Zack asked, "How so?" while eyeing the golden brown muffin, bursting with ripe blueberries, which Conan passed his way.

Nodding to his sister, who had reverted back to frowning, Conan explained, "Mom and Dad are moving. They needed somewhere to stay for two weeks and since Wynn just got this place, I convinced them she was a better choice than me." He flashed a wide, unapologetic grin.

Wynn huffed. "Not that I don't love my parents, but when you meet them you'll understand why I'm considering wringing Conan's neck."

Zack didn't want to meet her parents. He hadn't even wanted to meet her. With any luck, from here on out he'd successfully avoid the Lane clan altogether.

"But hey," Conan said, and punched Zack in the shoulder, nearly making him spill the distasteful coffee. "I like it that you wanted to protect her. Knowing she'll have a neighbor looking out for her makes me feel better about her living alone."

Conan had fists like sledgehammers, and not enough sense to temper his blows. The muscle in Zack's shoulder leaped in pain. He refused to show any weakness by rubbing it.

And he refused to become Wynn's protector, though God knew with a smart and loud mouth like hers, she'd likely need a battalion to shield her from retaliation. But before he could find words to express his thoughts, Dani appeared. She hesitated, showing unaccustomed shyness, her soft-bristled brush clutched in one hand, the other on the screen door.

Setting aside his coffee, Zack held out his hand and she skipped to him. He put her on his knee and began brushing her silky hair. "Dani, Conan is Wynn's brother."

Dani leaned close to his ear and whispered loudly enough for the birds in the trees to hear, "What do I call 'em?"

Wynn answered for him. "Well neighbors can't very well stand on formality, now can they? So, if you don't mind us calling you Dani, you can just call us Wynn and Conan. Deal?"

Dani twisted, stuck out her hand, and said, "Deal."

Conan laughed and enfolded the diminutive fingers with his massive paw. Muscles flexed and rolled along his arm, yet Zack couldn't help but notice that he was very gentle.

After Wynn shook Dani's hand, too, Dani stated, "Your hair looks funny."

"Dani." Her habit of speaking her mind was often humorous, but this wasn't one of those times.

She blinked at her father uncertainly. "It doesn't?"

It did, so what could he say? He settled on, "You know better than to be rude."

Far from insulted, Wynn laughed out loud and shook her head so more corkscrew curls sprang wild. "It feels funny, too. Wanna see?"

Dani looked at Zack for permission, and he could only shrug. Never in his life had he known a woman who behaved as she did, so how was he supposed to know how to deal with her?

Dani reached out, nearly falling off Zack's knee, and put her fingertips to the bouncing curls. She gave a tentative stroke, and then another. Her brow furrowed in concentration. "It's soft." And then to Zack, "Feel it, Daddy."

Zack nearly choked. "Uh, no, Dani..."

Conan must have had a wicked streak, because he taunted, "Ah, go ahead, Zack. Wynonna won't mind."

"Wynonna will loosen your jaw if you don't stop calling me *Wynnona!*"

Dani laughed. Zack was a little bemused to realize his daughter recognized the lack of threat in their repartee while he'd been alarmed by it.

"My name's Daniella, but no one calls me that. 'Cept Dad sometimes when he's mad."

Wynn gave a theatrical gasp. "Your father gets mad at you?" she teased, holding one hand to her chest. "Whatever for? Why, you're such a little angel."

Dani shrugged. "Not all the time. Sometimes I get into mis...mis..."

"Mischief," Zack supplied, "and don't make me sound like an ogre to our new neighbors."

She beamed at him. "He's the best dad in the whole world."

"Much better." Zack smiled and kissed her soft plump cheek. "She has her moments, and if angels can be rowdy and rambunctious, then the description does fit."

Conan laughed, but Wynn gave him another of those tender, intent looks. He frowned and turned away.

"You don't really fight with Conan," Dani told Wynn, as if Wynn might not be aware of that fact herself.

"I would never take a chance on hurting him," Wynn boasted. Then, pretending to share a confidence, she added, "Besides, he's my brother and I love him."

Dani sat back against her father's chest and crossed her arms. "I want a brother."

Zack choked.

Conan handed him a napkin, again staving off the awkward moment. "If you want to hear the real joke about Wynn's hair," Conan said, "then you should know that our father is a coiffeur."

"What's that?" Dani asked.

"A coiffeur," Wynn explained, "is just another word for a hairdresser."

Again and again, they took him by surprise, Zack thought. "That's...interesting," he remarked, and gulped down more of the awful vanilla coffee.

Wynn chuckled. "The fact that I won't let him touch my hair makes him crazy. Which is why I won't let him touch it, of course. Every time he sees me, he wails like he's in pain."

"And when she says wails, she means wails." Conan sipped his own coffee before setting the cup aside. "My dad is likely to be the only flaming heterosexual you'll ever meet."

Zack stared. *Flaming heterosexual?* Did these two

know any normal or mundane conversational tidbits? Couldn't they go on about the weather or something? Together, they were the strangest people he'd ever met so he had no doubt the parents had to be beyond odd as well. He kept silent.

His daughter did not.

"Does that mean hairdresser, too?" Dani asked.

Wynn quickly swallowed her bite of muffin. "No, Dani, that means he likes to dress in silk and lots of gold chains and he has this enormous diamond earring."

Oh Lord, Zack thought, and wished he could escape.

"Our mother, on the other hand, is the original hippie. She's into all things natural and doesn't wear any jewelry at all except for a plain wedding band."

"But," Conan interjected, casting a sly look at Wynn, "she loves my father enough to let him keep her hair trimmed."

"Daddy would have a heart attack if I asked him to do my hair now. You know that. Besides, he likes to have something to gripe at me about."

"Does your mom's hair look like yours?" Zack heard himself ask, curious despite himself.

"Heavens no! I got my hair from some long-deceased ancestor."

Conan leaned forward in a conspiratorial manner. "And believe me, we're all beyond grateful that he is long deceased."

Wynn shoved at him. "My father's hair is brown and sleek, and my mother's hair is blond like Conan's, but longer—all the way to her waist."

Dreading the answer, Zack asked, "When are they supposed to join you?"

"Next week," she mumbled, sounding despondent and resigned. "And I was so looking forward to living on my own."

"You lived at home until now?" As Zack asked that, he finished brushing the tangles from Dani's hair, smoothed it back and expertly wrapped the covered band around it, securing it in place. She bobbed her head a bit, making the ponytail bounce, then smiled and kissed him again. Zack gave her an affectionate squeeze—and noticed the silly smiles on his neighbors' faces.

He now felt conspicuous, all because he'd fixed his daughter's hair. It was no big deal, nothing elaborate, just a ponytail. And it wasn't like there was someone else to do it. Anything his daughter needed, he supplied. Except female company, but he was working on that.

"No," Wynn said, still looking too soft and female and approving, which for her was a gross contradiction. The contrast...intrigued him.

No, it did not!

"At twenty-eight," she continued, oblivious to his inner turmoil on her femaleness, "I've been out of the house for awhile. But I had two roommates, and they were both awful slobs. I'm sort of what you'd call..."

"Fanatical," Conan supplied, toasting her with his coffee cup. "She likes to keep an immaculate, organized house. Drives me crazy."

"Dad's fatical, too," Dani told them. "Mick and Josh tell him he'll make a good husband for some lucky woman some day."

"Is that right?" Amused, Conan eyed Zack.

Wynn drank more coffee, cleared her throat as if embarrassed, and finally put her cup aside. "Well, I can't stand having things thrown just anywhere. Busy people need to be organized."

Since Zack felt the same way, he could empathize with her. Other than Dani's toys, which he left scattered around so Dani wouldn't feel stifled, he liked to have a place for everything and everything in its place. He kept the house clean and once a month a service came to do a more thorough job, getting the baseboards and the ceiling and the air ducts—all the places he seldom had time to tend to.

The idea that they might have something in common was a little alarming, so he didn't belabor the point.

Dani slid off his lap to sit beside Wynn. She situated herself in the exact same pose as the neighbor, shoulders back, spine straight, head tilted just so. Except that Dani's legs hanging over the edge of the padded settee didn't even come close to touching the ground, while Wynn's not only touched, they folded so sharply her knees were practically in her face. Zack shook his head. He'd never seen legs so long. Or so nicely shaped.

Dani gave Wynn a toothy grin, then picked up her bowl of cereal and dug in.

"Conan falls into the slob category." Wynn handed Dani a napkin almost without thought. Zack wondered if she was around children often, then decided it didn't matter to him one iota. "Which is probably why my folks decided to spend their two weeks with me. It's far too easy to get lost in his cluttered apartment. He keeps newspapers around for weeks, and there's always something rotting in his refrigerator."

Zack couldn't stop his shudder of revulsion. Watching him, Wynn nodded in perfect accord. "It's disgusting," she confirmed.

To change the subject, Conan asked, "What do you do for a living, Zack?"

Both he and his sister stared at Zack with expectant expressions.

Dani answered for him, saying around a mouthful of cereal and milk, "He saves peoples. He's a hero."

Settling back in her seat, Wynn slowly nodded. "Mmmm. I can see that." She eyed Zack up and down...and up again, letting her gaze linger here and there. He felt that interested gaze like a lick of fire and wanted to groan.

"Your dad," she said, "has all the right makings of a hero. Big, muscular, handsome and kind." And then with an impish, very intimate and inviting smile, "I'm glad he's my neighbor."

IT WAS THE most curious sensation, Wynn thought, as if her heart had started to boil the second she'd seen him. Then, when he'd held his daughter on his knee and patiently brushed her hair, her heart outright melted.

She'd never felt anything like it. She'd never seen anyone like him.

And she was all but bowled over with a mixed jumble of emotions.

Dani herself caused part of the effect; Wynn couldn't imagine a more adorable little girl than the one sitting primly beside her, milk on her upper lip and her riotous hair neatly contained in a bouncy ponytail. The child had an impish demeanor that proved she was both smart and precocious.

Most of the effect, though, came from Zack Grange. *Wowza.* She hadn't believed one man could carry such a sizzling emotional and physical wallop, but Zack did. He stood the smallest bit taller than she, maybe an inch at most. Which meant he must stand a flat six feet. Her height, however, apparently didn't distress him.

No, before he'd recalled himself, Zack had looked at her with male appreciation, and she liked it. A lot.

She wished she hadn't worn the bulky sweatshirt with the stretched out neckline and the hem that hung midway down her shorts. Her upper body was as toned as the rest of her, and she wondered how he'd look at her there.

When she'd first dressed, the early morning air had carried a nip, but she was nowhere near cool now. In fact, she felt a little overheated. Maybe downright hot.

She guessed Zack to be around thirty, given the age of his daughter and his overall physique. It was his physique that had her doing more than her fair share of ogling. The man was put together just fine.

He wasn't a muscle-bound behemoth like her brother, but lean and toned, with an obvious strength that was partly innate male, partly specialized training. His chest was wide, his shoulders wider. He had narrow hips, long straight legs and large, lean hands and feet. There was no fat on his middle, no slouch in his stance.

Light brown hair, bone straight and disheveled from being roused out of bed, complemented gentle, intense blue eyes. His brows and beard stubble were darker, his jaw hard and stubborn.

But it was when he looked at his daughter that his gorgeous blue eyes held the most impact.

Only seconds after seeing Zack, she'd wanted him. The man exuded raw sexuality tempered with gentleness and caring. A highly potent combination.

Being around him felt...comfortable, in a dozen different ways.

With an acquaintance not quite an hour long, she knew enough to respect him. She'd already learned that he loved his daughter, was a natural defender of women, and showed politeness even when rude neighbors pulled him from a much-needed sleep.

She sighed, earning a strange look from both men and Dani.

"Sorry," she mumbled, wishing she could crawl over onto his lap now that Dani was no longer in it. But a big hulking girl like herself didn't sit in laps. In fact, she couldn't remember the last time a man had held her. "So what title applies to your heroic deeds, Zack?"

He rubbed his hands over his tired eyes while explaining. "I'm an EMT paramedic. Dani thinks Mick, Josh and I are all heroes. Actually I believe she has Mick's wife, Delilah, in that category now, too."

"They're heroes," Dani insisted with a child's love and devotion.

And Zack responded, "Don't talk with your mouth full, sweetheart."

"So you drive an ambulance, huh?" Conan leaned forward with interest. "Who do you work for?"

"The fire department. Josh is a fireman there. We've known each other forever."

Wynn tipped her head, recalling the other name he had mentioned. "And Mick? What does he do?"

"Mick is a cop. His wife, Delilah Piper-slash-Dawson is a—"

"Novelist!" Conan finished for him, surging to the edge of his seat with excitement. "Are you kidding me? You know Delilah Piper?"

"Don't forget the 'slash-Dawson' part or Mick will have your head." Zack grinned, showing even white teeth and a dimple in his left cheek. *A dimple!* Wynn's melting heart thumped so hard, she nearly missed the rest of Zack's explanation. "Since she and Mick married, he's been understanding about her name already being well known. He's proud of her career, but insistent that those of us who are familiar remember she's a married woman now."

"Possessive, is he?" Wynn asked.

And Conan said, "Are you nuts? She's *Delilah Piper*." He snorted. "I'd be possessive, too."

"You always are," Wynn said with a shake of her head. Her brother drove his present girlfriend crazy with his possessive, overbearing ways.

"I take it you're a fan?" Zack asked.

"I just finished her newest. That scene at the river was incredible."

"I can get your books signed for you if you want."

Wynn watched in disgust as her muscle-bound brother looked ready to get up and dance a jig. She glanced at Dani, and they shared a woman-to-woman smile. Dani even shook her head and rolled her big blue eyes, causing Wynn to chuckle.

While the men continued to work out the details of the books, Wynn turned to Dani. "So you're close to Josh and Mick and Delilah?"

"She wants to be called Del, only Mick won't. I think it's jus' to tease her."

"And Mick and Josh?"

"They're fun. Josh has lots of ladies, but he says none of 'em are prettier than me so he can't marry 'em."

"Smart man."

"Yeah." She nodded with a look of pity for the poor unwed Josh and the not-pretty-enough women. "Dad wants to get married, too, but he's gotta find a wife first." Dani scrunched up her face, studying Wynn.

Wynn squirmed under such close scrutiny. *From a child!* Luckily, Dani whispered to her father that she had to go in to the potty. After she went in, Zack returned to his conversation about Del Piper, keeping Conan enthralled.

Wynn looked at Zack. So, he wanted a wife, huh? Or was that something Dani had misconstrued?

How in the world was it that he hadn't already remarried? A man like Zack probably had women by the dozens. But then...she rethought that and shook her head at herself. Zack was very dedicated to his daughter, and she knew EMTs worked long shifts, sometimes up to sixty hours a week. That wouldn't leave him much time for dating, much less cultivating a lasting relationship.

He must have felt her gaze, for he glanced at her while Conan waxed poetic about Ms. Piper's remarkable talent. Their gazes met and held and Zack frowned. He glanced away, then back again. Wynn blinked at him, feeling soft and hot and excited.

She stared, knew she stared, and couldn't seem to help herself. Zack shifted, glaring at her then crossing one ankle over a knee.

He had thick ankles. And wrists. And long fingers and...one thought led to another and she couldn't keep herself from peeking at his lap. His jeans were old and faded and appeared very soft. They cupped him lovingly, outlining a bulge that proved most noticeable, even without him being aroused.

Her heart dropped into her stomach and began jumping erratically. Her palms tingled, craving to touch him, to weigh him in her hands—

"Stop that!"

She blinked hard and looked up at him. Conan went silent, confused. A red flush crept up Zack's neck. He cleared his throat and stood.

"The coffee and muffins were great. Thanks."

As dismissals went, it wasn't the least bit subtle, but Conan didn't seem to find anything amiss. He shook Zack's hand, saying, "I'll bring the books to you soon, if you're sure she won't mind signing them."

"Delilah's great. She won't mind." Zack didn't look at Wynn at all, and she had the feeling his avoidance was deliberate. But then, he'd caught her staring at his crotch, all but salivating.

She blushed. She'd known the man one hour, and already she'd behaved like a shameless hussy. Or worse, like a desperate spinster.

Oh God! Maybe that was how he saw her. After all, she was twenty-eight and single. The only male helping her move in was her brother; no fiancé, not even a boyfriend. He couldn't know that it was by choice, because she hadn't yet met a guy who...made her blood sing, not like he did.

Damn, damn, damn.

Not being of a shy or withdrawn nature, she stuck out her hand, daring him to continue ignoring her. She wouldn't allow it.

His jaw locked. With a false smile pinned to his tired face, he took her hand. His touch, his look, was beyond impersonal, and she hated it. "Welcome to the neighborhood, Wynn."

"Thanks." He tried to take his hand back, but she held on. "I'm sure we'll be seeing each other again."

After she said it, she winced. It sounded like a threat! Then she realized he was trying to tug his hand free and here she was, doing the macho 'grip' thing. Good God, she was making things worse by the second.

She turned him loose and put her hands in her pockets so she wouldn't be tempted to get hold of him again. Conan gathered up the carafe and the muffin plate.

Feeling like an idiot, she said, "Well, thanks again. And really, I am sorry we woke you."

Dani bounded back outside, then skidded to a disappointed halt. "You can't leave."

Zack put his hand on the top of her silky head. "I'm sure Wynn wants to finish unpacking, sweetheart. And you and I are going shopping."

Dani groaned, wilted, all in all acting like a child being sent to the woodshed.

Barely hiding a smile, Zack said, "None of that. We'll have lunch out and it'll be fine. You'll see."

Conan gave a crooked grin. "I gather she doesn't like shopping?"

"Not for clothes, no. But she's about worn out everything warm she has."

"Sounds like Wynn. She hates shopping, too."

Dani's eyes widened. "You do?"

Wynn shrugged. "I know it's supposed to be a girl thing, but I've never understood it. Thank goodness I don't need a lot of clothes."

Conan leaned forward. "She used to outgrow her

wardrobe daily, but we're hoping she's done growing by now."

Wynn elbowed him, caught Zack's look of disapproval, and wanted to throttle her brother. Zack didn't approve of their physical sparring, and she'd meant to cease it in front of him. But Conan had a way of egging her on. "I quit growing ten years ago. And with my job, casual clothes are perfect."

"What do you do?" Zack asked, then looked like he wanted to bite his tongue off.

"I'm a physical therapist. I work two days a week at the high school, two days a week at the college." She nodded toward her brother. "Conan owns a gym and I sometimes help out there, too, when the bodybuilders overdo it."

Zack looked dubious, but nodded. He said to Conan, again ignoring her, "A gym, huh?"

"Small, but it's all mine and I'm a good trainer. I do a lot of private stuff." He winked. "The clientele is as much female as male."

Bristling at Zack's disregard and her brother's caveman attitude, Wynn said, "Rachael will get you if she hears that particular leer in your tone."

Conan shrugged, unconcerned with the warning. "Rachael is my current girlfriend, not my wife. And speaking of Rachael, I should get going." He gave one last wave and headed off.

Wynn gazed after him, watching him go down the steps and then around the porch toward her new house. She sighed. "Me, too. I've got a lot of unpacking to do yet." She turned to Zack, who appeared anxious to finish the goodbyes. "Being as we're neighbors," she thought to say, "feel free to borrow if you ever need to. You know, the proverbial cup of sugar or whatever."

"Thanks." Zack's tone was dry. "I'll keep that in mind. And thanks for the coffee and muffins. They were...great."

With nothing left to say, Wynn stepped off the porch with a lagging step. "Okay, well...bye."

"Goodbye, Wynn."

She glanced over her shoulder to see Zack escaping into his house. He closed the door behind him, and she heard the lock click. Well, hell. His goodbye had sounded entirely too final.

That just wouldn't do. She wanted him. One way or another.

3

"LOOK DAD!"

Zack pulled the car into the driveway and put it in park. He didn't want to look. Because of the direction Dani pointed, he already knew what—or rather who—he'd see. And he wanted to keep her out of his mind, not dwell on her further. He'd done enough dwelling.

All day long, his mind had wandered to her, and he didn't like it. Even while buying miniature jeans with butterflies sewn on the pockets, and lace-up brown boots meant for a boy that had his daughter begging for them, he'd thought of Wynn. While hauling armloads of shopping bags filled with pastel sweatshirts and soft sweaters and long sleeved T-shirts, he'd remembered the way Wynn had stared at him—*where she'd stared at him*—and he'd been distracted.

Not just distracted, but edgy with a sort of vague arousal.

Well, not really vague, either. More like...acute.

Damn, damn, damn.

He'd been forced to fight himself all day. And all that did was add to his exhaustion and detract from the pleasure he usually enjoyed while spending special time with Dani.

He'd pictured Wynn in his mind as they ate lunch in the food court, and he'd missed most of the matinee movie because his brain not only conjured what had already transpired, but what might yet come if he were to be friendlier to her.

And that wouldn't do! She was a neighbor living right behind him, so anything casual, *like hot gritty, satisfying sex*, was out of the question. And anything less casual, like friendship, would only make him want the sex more.

Wynn came nowhere near meeting his requirements for involvement, so it'd be best if he stayed clear of her altogether.

"Dad, *look*."

Dani, with her insistent, squeaky voice, gave him little choice. Zack glanced up to where she pointed, even as he said, "We need to get all these clothes put away..." His words died as he took in the sight of Wynn, now wearing a soft beige halter top, struggling with a long flat box. His driveway was at the side of his house, leading to an attached garage, which gave him a clear view of her house. Her yard was now empty of the packing boxes; it was the huge department store box that held her attention. Zack couldn't see the picture on the box to determine what she'd bought, but then, he wasn't exactly focused on the box.

Beneath the hot early-evening sun, Wynn's broad, toned shoulders looked dewy with perspiration and flexed with feminine muscles. Her belly... He swallowed hard. Her belly was flat, taut with her straining efforts, her waist lean and supple, dipping and curving. She looked sexy and healthy and strong and so utterly female his muscles cramped.

The effect of those long legs had nearly been his undoing that morning. Now seeing her upper parts more bare than covered was enough to make him sweat along with her. He just adored female bellies, and hers was especially enticing.

He felt Dani's hand on his arm and managed to wipe away the gleam of lust before looking down at her.

"You should help her," Dani declared.

Oh, no. Zack had no intention of getting anywhere near Wynn. He shook his head and finished undoing Dani's car seat. By age, Dani was old enough to forego the special seat, but by size... His daughter was so petite it'd probably be another year before he felt comfortable with only a seat belt for her protection. "We've got our own work to do, Dani."

But no sooner did he have his daughter free from the seat than she opened the car door and slithered out. "Hello Wynn!" She waved both arms, drawing the neighbor's attention.

Wynn stopped struggling with the box and looked up. She wiped a forearm across her brow, squinted in their direction, then broke out in a smile. Even from the distance, Zack could see the open welcome in that smile.

He cursed, but silently.

Cutting across the yards, Wynn headed toward them.

He wanted to groan. He wanted to ignore her and go inside.

He wanted sex, damn it. With her.

No.

"Hey you two!" She stopped by Dani's side of the car, hands on her hips, legs braced apart. "How'd the shopping go?"

Dani tipped her head way back to grin up at Wynn. "We bought lots of stuff. And we saw a movie, too."

Wynn automatically went to her knees. Zack remembered her doing that earlier, too, when she'd spoken with Dani. Was it an allowance she made for her height? A man wouldn't be expected to do that, but a woman?

Or did she just like kids enough that she wanted to greet them on an eye level?

"A whole new wardrobe, huh? Terrific." She glanced up at Zack. Her hazel eyes looked warm and welcoming, even intimate, at least to his overeager imagination. "Got it all taken care of?" she asked.

He cleared his throat. His brain was already in sexual overdrive, his body too long deprived, and now Wynn got on her knees in front of him. Her face, her beautiful mouth, were level with... No. It was too much.

Zack turned away and began yanking bags out of the car. "She should be all set for fall."

"I went shopping, too," Wynn told him, her voice now sounding confused by his dismissal. "I bought a hammock for the backyard."

Zack froze with his arms loaded down. Slowly he

turned to face her. "A hammock?" Surely she didn't expect to lounge around in a hammock. Not where he could see her? "Where do you intend to put it?"

She pointed. "Those are the only two trees big enough and close enough together to work. I always wanted a hammock, almost as much as I wanted my own house. After I finished unloading boxes, I couldn't resist. This weather is perfect for lying around outside and reading or napping."

A thousand questions went winging through his mind, but he heard himself ask, "You went shopping in *that?*" The way he was staring at her halter, which looked far too enticing molded over soft, heavy breasts that were in perfect proportion to the rest of her big body, he knew she knew just what he meant.

Then when he realized what had come out of his unruly mouth, and how incredibly possessive he'd sounded, he quickly added, "You're talking about in *my* trees?" Both yards had an abundance of shade, but the trees she'd pointed at were the ones edging his property.

She'd be right there, visible to him, flaunting herself to him, wearing on his determination. He couldn't handle it. He'd never had a problem with temptation before, but he'd never met Wynn before, either.

She blinked those awesome hazel eyes at him, and even that seemed provocative, deliberate. Hell, her breathing seemed designed to drive him nuts.

Her expression intent, watchful, she came to her feet. He didn't mean to, but his gaze switched to her legs, then quickly lifted back to her belly. She wasn't overly muscular there, not in the least mannish, just very smooth and lithe and softly rounded just as a woman should be.

His heart punched into his ribs.

Hands on her naked waist, one hip cocked out enticingly, she waited for his gaze to finally rise up to hers. It took him far too long to get there, but then, she had a lot of skin showing.

When their eyes met, Wynn smiled, but there was nothing friendly in the tilt of her lips or the narrowing of her eyes. "I changed when I got home," she informed him, "before getting the box out of the car. And the trees are actually mine. I specifically asked before buying the house. The Realtor checked the property line just to be sure."

Zack wanted to howl. He wanted to tell her that he didn't give a damn about the trees or whom they belonged to. He wanted to put his daughter down for a nap, then drag his neighbor off to bed—or to the floor or the ground or against one of those stupid trees...

He managed his own strained smile. "I see."

Dani, not understanding the sudden tension between the adults, reached up to tug on the hem of Wynn's shorts. "We got pizza for dinner."

Wynn's smile was genuine when she looked at his daughter. "Sounds like you've had a wonderful day." She ruffled Dani's hair, then saluted Zack. "I better get back to work. I want to get the hammock set up."

"You can eat with us!"

Zack cursed softly at his daughter's invitation, but not softly enough. Wynn heard.

Even though her chin lifted and her eyes were direct, she looked hurt. And that hurt *him*. Damn it, he didn't want to insult her, but neither did he want to be further forced into her company.

"Thanks sweetie," Wynn said to Dani though she continued to look at Zack, "but I've got too much to do."

"Don't you like pizza?" Dani asked, stubborn to the core and always determined to get her own way.

"I do, but it's been a busy day, and I'm not done yet. Maybe another time, okay?"

Wynn turned away and almost stumbled. For the first time, Zack noticed the weariness in her long limbs, the slight droop to those surprisingly wide, proud shoulders.

Suspicion bloomed, with it annoyance. Using the same tone that always worked for his daughter, Zack uttered, "Wynn."

She paused, turned to face him with one brow raised.

He stared at her face and noticed the exhaustion. Damn it. "When did you eat last?"

"What?" She couldn't have looked more confused by his inquiry. Beside him, Dani all but jiggled with excitement. She knew her father too well and knew he'd just made up his mind.

"Did you have lunch?" Zack demanded, and got a blank expression. He sighed. "Have you eaten anything since the muffins and coffee this morning?"

Rather than answer him, Wynn replied, "I appreciate your concern, Zack, but I'm sure you've got more important things to do than keep track of my meals." Again, she turned away.

He should just let her go, Zack thought, watching her leave and doing his best to keep his gaze off her ample and well-shaped rear end. But his daughter watched him with a look she'd probably picked up from him, one that showed extreme disappointment in his behavior. Dani no doubt expected him to rectify his bad manners, and he knew he should. Even with the womanly sway to her hips, Wynn looked ready to drop, her feet dragging.

She'd been neighborly and friendly and he'd been a surly jerk. All because he hadn't had a woman in too long and she appealed to him on some insane yet basic level. That couldn't be blamed on her.

Zack bent low and said to Dani, "Start carrying the bags up to the porch and I'll be right back."

With a severe look, Dani ordered, "Talk her into eatin' with us."

He sighed. "I'll try."

Dani pushed against him. "Go! Before she's all the way home."

Wynn had nearly made it before Zack reached her. She had to have heard his approach, but she ignored him. He caught her arm and turned her around to face him. "Wait a minute."

Seeing he was alone, she barked, *"What now?"*

He couldn't help it. He smiled, then actually laughed.

"Without Dani listening, I get the full brunt of your temper? Is that it?"

"Don't kid yourself." She looked furious and still hurt. Pushing her wild hair out of her face, she sneered, "If you had my full temper, you'd be flat on your back right now."

Her threat brought with it an image of him on his back, her over him, riding him slow and deep. Her legs were so long and so strong he had no doubt her endurance would be endless, mind-blowing. He glanced down at her breasts, thinly covered by the soft material of the halter. Without his mind's permission, he imagined them naked, her nipples puckered, begging for his fingers, his mouth. Her chest glistened from the heat, her skin was radiant and so very soft looking.

No words came, no reply, but she must have read his mind because she drew back and her anger melted away. "I didn't mean that," she whispered in a shaky voice.

He couldn't stop himself from asking, "Mean what?"

She hesitated, their gazes locked, then she shrugged with a blatant challenge. "Sex. That's what you were thinking. Though I suppose you'll deny it now."

Zack rubbed his face. "No, I won't deny it." His neck and shoulders were still sore from the night before, when he'd dealt with two very unusual crises, and now his body throbbed with sexual tension. "Look, Wynn..."

"Hey, I understand. Dani is a sweetheart, but kids

have a way of speaking out of turn. No harm done, and I really do have plenty more work to do."

He dismissed what she said to ask, "You've been working all day, haven't you? I bet you haven't eaten at all except for that muffin at dawn."

"It wasn't exactly dawn—"

"Close enough."

"—and my eating habits aren't your concern."

Why did he have to have the most frustrating woman in creation move in behind him? Why did he have to find her so appealing that even his teeth were aroused? He was tired, achy, sexually frustrated, and now he had to deal with this.

Knowing Dani would only show so much patience before she decided to come help him out, he admitted, "I want you. That's why I was rude."

Those golden eyes opened so wide, she looked comical. He heard her swallow. Her mouth opened, but nothing came out.

Zack looked toward the trees where she planned to hang her hammock. "Between Dani and work, I don't get a lot of chances to date and it's been a long time— too damn long—since I've been with a woman. I didn't get enough sleep last night or I'd probably show better restraint today, but I'm running on four hours tops, and all my understanding and restraint is saved up for my daughter."

She said, "Oh."

"I don't want you to worry that I'm going to come on to you—"

"I'm not worried," she rushed to assure him.

"—because I have no intention of doing that."

She said, "Oh," again. This time with regret, if his tired ears didn't deceive him.

"Yeah, oh." He shook his head. "Come and eat with us, then I'll help you get that box to the backyard and from there we can be sociable, but not overly friendly. Okay?"

"Not overly friendly," she repeated, "because you don't want to want me?"

"That's right." Talking about it wasn't helping. He felt like an ass, more so with every word that left his mouth. "It wouldn't be a good idea what with us being neighbors and everything."

"I see."

She looked perplexed. Zack sighed again and looked around to see his daughter watching intently, arms crossed and foot tapping. He turned back to Wynn. "You understand, surely. Being neighbors is one thing. But it could get awkward if we took it any further than that."

She nodded. "Awkward."

His eyes narrowed at her patronizing tone. "That's right. Relationships have a way of complicating things, especially if they don't work out, and since I'm not looking to get involved—"

"It couldn't work out?" She smiled. "Well, you got me there."

What in the world did she have to smile about? *He*

wasn't amused. In fact, he was getting close to annoyed. "We'd still be living next door to each other."

"I'm sure not planning on moving!"

"And then we'd both—"

"Feel awkward." She gave a sage nod. "I see your point."

Zack ground his teeth. "Will you join us for pizza or not?"

She licked her lips and tilted her head. "Can I clarify something first?"

"Make it quick. Dani will be on us any minute now."

"I'm standing here all sweaty and hot and my hair looks worse than usual and yet...you say I'm turning you on?"

Zack wanted to throttle her. Not wanting to hurt her feelings, he'd tried being honest with her, and now she felt free to provoke him.

She did look hot and sweaty—like she'd just been making love most vigorously. He stiffened his resolve. "Let's not belabor the point, okay?"

"Okay." She searched his face. "I just wanted to be sure."

Together they started back toward Dani. Zack could feel the heat of Wynn at his side, could smell the intensified scent of sun-kissed feminine skin, of shampoo and lotion and woman.

"How long's it been?" she asked with unparalleled nonchalance, as if that wasn't the most personal topic around.

Of course, he'd brought it up. He didn't look at her. "Long enough."

"For me, too." She smiled toward Dani and waved. "Although I don't think that's why you turn me on." She glanced at him, her long lashes at half-mast, her lips slightly curled. She leaned closer and breathed into his ear, "I think it's your gorgeous bod that's doing the trick."

Zack stumbled over his own feet, which left him standing behind Wynn. She walked over to his yard, took Dani's hand, and together they marched around front to the porch. He heard Dani say, "I can show you my new clothes!"

And Wynn replied happily, "Right after we eat. I'm starved."

WYNN FINISHED OFF her fourth slice of pizza and sighed. She hadn't realized she was so hungry until she'd taken the first bite. Then she'd had to be careful not to make a glutton of herself. "That was heavenly. Thank you."

Zack just grunted, but Dani said, "You ate as much as Dad."

"Not true! He had one piece more than me." Then, eyeing Zack, she added, "But he has a lot more muscle so he naturally needs more to eat."

Zack choked on the drink of cola he'd just taken, and slanted her an evil look. It was all she could do not to laugh.

He wanted her.

He didn't want to want her, but he did. That was a good start. She could work with that.

On her end, she was crazy-nuts about him already. Not only was the man handsome and well built, but he had a soft streak for his daughter, an outrageous honesty, and his house was spotless. She'd never known a bachelor who enjoyed cleanliness as much as she did.

"Your house is set up different from mine." She looked around, admiring the orderliness of it.

Zack lounged back in his seat. "It's basically the same, I just had a few walls taken out to open things up."

She'd have done the same if she could afford it, but for now, having her own home more than satisfied her. "It's bigger, too."

He shrugged. "Not by that much. I added on to the dining room when I got the hot tub, and had the patio doors put in."

Wynn had noticed the large hot tub right away. It sat outside his dining room, to the left of his kitchen at the edge of the patio, and was partially shielded by a privacy fence.

The sliding doors really made the dining room bigger and brighter. Her house only had the one kitchen door that opened to the side yard. Wynn had noticed that from Zack's kitchen or his patio doors, he could look at the entire side view of her house, and see into her front and backyard. The only thing that would obstruct his view were the trees.

This topic didn't have him grinding his teeth, so she

pursued it. "The landscaping in the back is gorgeous."
He had as many mature trees as she had, with one especially large tree close to the house. Long branches
reached over the roof and shaded the kitchen from the
afternoon sun. Zack had hung a swing from one of
those sturdy branches for Dani.

Around the patio, he had a lot of lush ground cover
and shade-loving flowers bright with color. It took a remarkable man to plant flowers, but then she'd already
made that assessment about him.

"Thank you. I needed the covered deck so we could
get to the tub in the winter without plodding through
the snow."

"You use it when it's cold?" Imagining Zack mostly
naked and wet made her tongue stick to the roof of her
mouth. It'd be great if he offered to share, but she
wouldn't hold her breath.

He shrugged. "Off and on all year."

Wynn cleared her throat and steered her mind to
safer imaginings. "I like the way you've decorated. It's
nice and casual and comfortable." Everything was done
in mellow pine with shades of cream and greens. There
were a few plants, lots of pictures of Dani, and a couple
of photos she assumed to be of his deceased wife. The
woman was pretty, fair like Dani, but with longer hair.
She looked very young, and Wynn made a point of not
looking at the photos too long, despite her curiosity; she
didn't want to dredge up bad memories for Zack. When
she asked him about his wife, it would be without Dani
listening.

"Can Wynn and me be excused now?"

Zack said, "May Wynn and I. And yes, you may. Wash your hands first, though."

Dani ran to the sink, used the three-step stool in front of it, and turned on the water. Over her shoulder, she said to Wynn, "My stuff's in my room."

Wynn watched Zack push back his chair. He didn't quite look at her. "I'll go carry that box to the backyard for you while Dani shows you her new clothes." He paused beside Dani, bent and kissed the top of her head. "I'll be right back, okay?"

She nodded. "Okay."

He went out the kitchen door and was gone before Wynn could agree or disagree.

When Dani dragged Wynn upstairs, she got a peek at the rest of his house. There wasn't a speck of dust anywhere. Not that she was looking for dust, but the complete and total lack of it was evident, and impressive.

Everything was neat and orderly, except for Dani's toys scattered here and there. She noticed two pine chests in the family room, one opened to reveal an assortment of dolls and games inside. The top of a desk was littered with crayons and construction paper and safety scissors.

She passed Zack's bedroom at the top of the stairs and, hoping Dani wouldn't notice, she peered in. More polished, heavy pine furniture filled the moderate size room. The bed was made up with a rich, dark-brown down comforter. A slight breeze wafted in through the open window, through which Wynn could just see

Zack, in the corner of her yard, the large box hefted onto his shoulder.

They were of a similar height, but the difference in their strength was notable, and arousing. The box had been heavy and cumbersome to her, yet Zack handled it as if it weighed no more than a sack of flour.

She watched him for a long moment before it dawned on her that if she could see him now, he could see her...anytime she was in the yard.

She asked Dani, "Is this where you and your dad were when we first said hello, today?"

"Yeah, 'cept Dad was still in his underwear then 'cuz he'd just woke up."

"I see." Boy, did she see. Not wanting to give away her interest by lingering, she allowed Dani to hustle her along to her room. This time the furniture was white, with a pale yellow spread and yellow-striped wallpaper on the bottom half of the wall, topped by a white chair rail. An enormous corkboard hung behind the bed, filled to overflowing with pictures Dani had drawn.

With Dani's bedroom on the same side of the house as Zack's, Wynn was tempted to peek out the window again. Instead, she concentrated on the multitude of bags tossed onto Dani's bed.

When Dani began pulling out the clothes, Wynn couldn't help but laugh. Other than small detailing here and there, the clothes could have been for a boy. No frills for Dani, evidently. Wynn approved.

She and Dani spent a good fifteen minutes looking at

everything, paying special attention to a tiny pair of rugged lace-up brown boots that would look adorable on Dani's small feet.

Wynn commented on Dani's obvious artistic talent, after which Dani determined to draw Wynn a picture. Since she didn't want Wynn to watch, Wynn headed back downstairs. She found Zack in the kitchen, cleaning up the remains of their dinner. She picked up two glasses and carried them to the dishwasher. "I was going to help you with this."

"No need." He moved around her to the table and spent an inordinate amount of time crushing the pizza box.

It amused Wynn that he wouldn't look at her. She leaned back against the sink, her hands propped on the counter at either side of her hips. "It's the least I could do after imposing on you. Twice."

Again, he moved around her to the garage door. He put the garbage in a can, secured the lid, and came back in. "You were invited."

"Grudgingly."

Zack paused, rubbed the back of his neck, flexed as if trying to rid himself of tension. When he looked at her, his eyes were a very dark blue. "I explained that, Wynn."

"Indeed you did." She crossed her ankles and watched his gaze flicker toward her legs and back again. How odd for him to be attracted to her while she was such a wreck. Odd, but exciting. "About the hammock..."

"What about it?"

"If you don't want it in the trees, I can return it. We're neighbors and the last thing I want to do is cause any hard feelings. I realize the trees are almost smack-dab on the borderline."

He shook his head. "It's not a problem."

"That's not the impression I got when I mentioned it."

Head dropped forward, hands on his hips, he stopped. He stared at his feet for a long moment, then lifted his gaze to her face. "Look—"

The ringing of the phone made him pause. He took two almost angry strides to the phone on the wall and picked it up. "Hello?"

Wynn tried to look like she wasn't listening, but it was apparent he was speaking with a friend. The infamous husband to a famous novelist? The lady-killer Josh?

A lady-friend of his own?

She didn't like that idea at all, and went about wiping off the table, closing up the dishwasher. Zack watched her as he spoke casually, saying, "Sure, I could use the company. That'll work. All right, fifteen minutes." He hung up.

Dani bounded into the room, a colorful picture held in one hand. "Who was it?"

Zack scooped her up and held her to his chest. "Mick and Josh are coming over. If you want to get your bath a little early, you'll have time to visit before bed."

Mick and Josh must be very special to Dani, Wynn assumed, given the way her sweet face lit up.

She leaned around Zack to see the picture. "Is that for me?"

Suddenly looking shy, Dani said, "Yeah," and held it out. Zack looked at it first and chuckled. Then Wynn had it and she held it out, studying it.

Dani had drawn the two trees in the backyard, Wynn and her hammock. Wynn grinned when she saw that she and the trees were the same lofty height, and her hair was accurately portrayed as a tornado. "It's beautiful, Dani." She held the picture to her chest, curiously touched, and smiled. "I love it."

Dani laid her head on Zack's chest. "Really?"

With a strange lump in her throat, she nodded. "Really." Wynn wished she could hold the little girl, too, that she could be the recipient of that adoring hug. She'd never thought much about kids before, but now she did, and an insidious yearning filled her. "May I keep it?" she asked, feeling overly emotional. "I'd like to put it on my refrigerator so everyone who visits me can see it, too."

This pleased Dani a lot. "Okay." And with a distinct lack of subtlety, the little girl added, "I could even visit you and see it sometime."

One look at Zack told Wynn that he didn't consider it a good idea. Tough, she thought. There was no way she'd hurt Dani's feelings just because Zack had some strange hang-up about getting friendly with her.

Feeling defiant, she said, "I'd like that a lot."

And on impulse, she leaned over and kissed Dani's cheek. Zack reared back, well out of reach, but Wynn still felt the sizzle of being so close to him.

She told Dani goodbye, winked at Zack, and let herself out through the kitchen door.

The sun had almost completely set, leaving long shadows over the lawns. If she hoped to get her hammock up in time to enjoy it tonight, she'd have to get a move on. She went in her house first to retie her hair. It was forever in her face, making her nuts. She found her small box of tools and headed back out.

Fifteen minutes later, when she'd almost finished, she heard the car pull into Zack's driveway. Curiosity got the better of her, and she peered toward the house. A floodlight mounted over Zack's garage door lit the area. Wynn saw two men get out, both of them tall and handsome. One had dark coloring, like a fallen angel, and the other was a golden Adonis. Mick and Josh, she decided, and it was easy to figure out which was which.

Sheesh. Living next door to Zack-the-hunk would be hard enough without him having other impressive hunks over to distract her. She should have been immune to gorgeous men, considering she helped out at Conan's gym and saw well-built muscular guys every day, often in nothing more than skimpy shorts and athletic shoes. But these three...what a visual variety!

The golden one looked up just as she started to turn away, and he kept looking. *Busted!* He knew she'd been eyeing him and no doubt knew why. His type—tall, sexy, well-built and handsome to boot—expected female adoration.

His companion turned, too, then propped his hands on his hips and did his own share of staring. Good Lord, her first day in her own house and she kept making a spectacle of herself.

Seeing no hope for it, Wynn summoned up a friendly and hopefully casual wave, which both men returned. The dark one looked merely polite and curious, but the other watched her with interest.

A second later Zack's door opened and both men got yanked inside.

4

"GET AWAY FROM the damn window," Zack growled.

Josh, still holding aside the café drape on the small window over the kitchen sink, peered over his shoulder at Zack. "Who is she?"

"Nobody. Just a neighbor."

"She's Wynn." Dani, perched in royal splendor on Mick's thigh, showed none of her father's reservation. "She's our new neighbor."

Josh lifted a brow. "Is that right?"

"She had breakfast with us." Dani smiled after that statement.

Mick shared a look with Josh. "Breakfast, huh?"

Zack threw ice into three glasses. "Quit jumping to conclusions. She woke me up this morning, that's all."

Josh dropped the curtain and turned. "Long, tall and sexy got you out of bed, and you say that's *all*?"

Mick choked on a laugh.

Zack, after casting a quick glance at his daughter, scowled. Luckily Dani was busy singing and drawing Mick a picture, which Mick pretended to attend to when actually Zack knew he was soaking up every word. "It's not like that!" He caught himself, shocked at his own vehemence, and explained more calmly, "She and her brother were making a racket moving in. When she realized she'd awakened us, she brought over coffee and some muffins.''

"Nice neighbor," Josh muttered, and turned back to the window.

"She had pizza with us, too, and I drawed her a picture."

"Drew her a picture," Zack automatically corrected, and realized his daughter had been all ears after all. When she looked up at him, he thought to add, "A beautiful picture, honey."

She held up her newest endeavor. "This one is, too."

Mick leaned back to see it, pretending to dump Dani, which made her squeal. "It's incredibly beautiful," he confirmed. He hugged her close and kissed her cheek.

Zack shook his head. His daughter had more than her fair share of male role models. Now she needed a female role model—preferably one who wasn't loud and pushy and too damn big.

Josh said, "Damn, does she never stop working?"

"Not that I've noticed." Unable to keep himself from it, Zack went to the window and peeked out. "What's she doing?"

"Hanging a clothesline. Hell, the moon is out. She's working from the porch light."

Dani said quite seriously, "You cuss too much. Hell and damn are bad words."

Wincing, Josh muttered, "Sorry."

Zack had long ago explained to Dani that while grown men might say certain words now and then, she was still a little girl and was strictly forbidden to do the same. He forgot his daughter's bossiness as he watched Wynn go about her business. "What in the world is she hanging up?"

Josh narrowed his eyes. "Looks like her laundry. Like—" he smiled "—her underwear."

Mick came out of his chair in a rush and crowded into the window. Being that he still held Dani, it was a tight fit. He snorted. "You're both lechers. You should give the woman some privacy."

None of them moved.

Dani said, "We saw her butt today."

Both Josh and Mick turned to stare at him. Zack frowned, ready to explain, then he saw Wynn toss a nightgown over the line and clip it into place with a clothespin. It wasn't a sexy nightgown, but rather what appeared to be yards and yards of material. Course, for a woman her size, it'd take a lot of cloth to cover her.

For some stupid reason that thought made him smile.

Moonlight played over her flyaway hair and the slant of the porch light made exaggerated shadows on her body. Why was she hanging her laundry at night? For that matter, why hadn't she worn down yet? She'd been working all day, non-stop, and it was too damn distracting. The woman must have inexhaustible energy, and that thought did more than make him smile. It made him wonder how she might put all that energy to use.

Through the open window, they all heard her begin to whistle.

"This is pathetic," Mick groused. "You've got me here playing peeping Tom when I'd really rather be playing cards."

Josh explained, "That's because you're blissfully married and therefore immune to fantasies."

Zack glared at him. "Don't tell me you're interested in her?"

And before Josh could answer, Dani braced herself between Mick and Josh, leaned forward toward the screen, and yelled through the window, "Hello Wynn! We's peeping Toms!"

They all three ducked so fast, their heads smacked together.

Mick, on the floor with his back against the sink cabinet, flipped Dani upside down while laughing and said, "I ought to hang you by your toes for that!" He tickled her belly and they both laughed.

Josh looked at Zack and said, "Do you think she heard?"

"That one? She hears everything." Then to his daughter, "Sweetheart, you don't tell people when you're looking at them."

"Why not?"

Josh crept up the edge of the sink and peeked out. With a resigned expression he completely straightened and called out, "It's a little late to be doing laundry."

Realizing Wynn must have been looking toward the window, Zack stood, too. He heard her soft laugh, then, "My new washer and dryer won't arrive for a few more days. I needed clean stuff for tomorrow."

To Zack's disgruntlement, Josh smiled, walked to the kitchen door, and continued right on outside and around to Wynn's house. He should put up a damn privacy fence.

Dani pulled away from Mick and followed. Mick shrugged at Zack, hauled himself to his feet, and followed suit.

Groaning, forced into the situation he'd wanted most to avoid, Zack went along.

When Wynn saw them all approaching, she dropped an item of clothing back into her basket and walked to meet them halfway. Though the night had grown considerably cooler, she was still in the halter and shorts and Zack wanted to strip off his shirt and cover her with it. But it was too late. Josh had already seen her, and was already in charm mode.

Wynn held out her hand when he reached her. "Hello. Wynn Lane."

Josh took her hand, but not in a handshake. He held her fingers carefully, as if she were fragile. "Josh Marshall," he murmured, and his tone alone gave away his thoughts on seduction. "Nice to meet you."

Zack wanted to kick him.

Wynn tried to tug her hand free, but Josh wasn't being reasonable about it. She snuck a glance at Zack and then back to Josh. "You're the fireman, right?"

He looked briefly surprised, and Zack explained, "Dani told her all about both of you."

To Mick she said, "My brother is a big fan of your wife's work."

Mick reached out, took Josh's wrist and pried their hands apart, then indulged his own handshake. At least his was entirely casual and quick. "Mick Dawson. Nice to meet you, Wynn."

She looked at Zack. "I hope I wasn't disturbing you again?"

"We were peekin' at you," Dani informed her.

Wynn just laughed and petted her hand over Dani's hair in a show of affection that Zack felt clean down to his gut. "Well," she said with a wide smile, "I imagine anyone doing laundry by moonlight is sure to draw attention." And to Zack, "The thing is, I'm still too keyed up from moving in to relax, and I actually brought laundry with me from my apartment, so I figured I might as well get it done. Stuff dried on the line always smells so good, don't you think?"

Zack thought *she* smelled good. Working all day had intensified her natural scent, making it more potent, more intoxicating.

He snorted at his own ridiculous fancy and told her, "There's a Laundromat a couple of miles away, next door to the grocery."

"You could use our washer and dryer," Dani offered.

Feeling his smile freeze, Zack said, "Or you could use our washer and dryer."

Wynn was already shaking her head. "No, I don't mind using the line."

Josh stepped in front of Zack. "I'm not that far away. Feel free to use mine until yours arrive."

Zack considered strangling him. It wasn't that he

cared personally, because he *didn't*, but it'd be almost as awkward for Josh to get involved with her as it would be for Zack. Josh wasn't ready to settle down, and in fact, since Mick's wedding, he'd been overindulging in a big way. Zack did *not* want him overindulging with his neighbor.

Mick said, "If you're about done, we were just getting some drinks. You could join us."

She took a step back. "Oh no, but thanks anyway."

"Join us, join us!" Dani sang, bouncing up and down in renewed energy.

"You," Zack told his daughter, "are about to go to bed."

Before Dani could summon up a temper about that, Wynn said, "Actually, so am I."

All three men stared at her.

She cleared her throat. "That is, I need to get showered and..." She looked from one fascinated male gaze to the other and coughed. "I'm a mess. I've been working all day."

In a feminine gesture that took him by surprise, considering he hadn't seen much in the way of femininity from her, Wynn attempted to smooth her hair.

Josh tipped his head. "You look fine."

His voice was low and appreciative and again Zack wanted to strangle him.

"Her hair is soft," Dani informed Josh in a loud whisper, then poked him in the thigh.

"Is that right?" Showing none of the reserve Zack had exhibited, Josh reached out and fingered a bouncing curl at her temple before gently tucking it behind her ear. "You're right, Dani. It's very soft."

Wynn twittered and took another step away. "I've got to finish up here. But it was nice meeting you both. Dani, sweet dreams!"

Josh murmured low and suggestively, "You, too."

She gave another ridiculous, girlish twitter and turned to hurry away. Josh stood there, hands on his hips, watching her go with his gaze southerly enough to singe her backside, until Zack elbowed him. Hard.

They all trooped back into the kitchen, Josh rubbing his ribs as if he'd been mortally wounded. Dani now had her head on Mick's shoulder and she yawned. They were all three aware of how quickly Dani would collapse into a sound slumber, and they shared smiles.

Zack scooped his daughter into his arms. "Time for you to hit the sack, sweetie." Once Dani started fading, she went fast. She'd run right up until she ran out of gas.

She blinked sleepy eyes at Josh and Mick. "G'night."

Josh bent and kissed her nose. "Night princess."

Mick tickled her toes. "Good night, honey."

As Zack turned to leave the kitchen, he saw Mick sit at the table, and Josh go back to the open window. He grumbled under his breath as he hauled his small bundle upstairs. He was just lowering Dani to her mattress when she said in a low, drowsy voice, "Josh likes her."

Pausing, Zack said, "You think so?"

Dani nodded. "I like her, too. Don't you?"

"She's fine." Zack pulled the sheet up to Dani's chin,

smoothed her hair and kissed her forehead. That didn't suffice, so he kissed her again, then cuddled her close, squeezing her until she gave a protesting squeak. "I love you, baby."

"I love you, too, Daddy."

"Do you need to potty?"

"Nope." She rolled to her side, cushioned her cheek on one tiny fist, and let out a long deep breath.

With a last peck to her brow, Zack stood. Dani was already snoring softly. For a long minute, he just looked down at her. She was by far the most precious thing in the world to him. It seemed every time he looked at her it struck him anew how much he loved her. That she was his, a part of him, was beyond remarkable.

Josh was still at the damn window when Zack reentered the kitchen. "You look like a lovesick pup."

Mick choked on a laugh. "As compared to you, who's playing the part of the snarling junkyard dog?"

At Mick's taunting words, Zack paused, but only for a second. He knew his friends, and if they had half an inkling of how Wynn affected him, he'd never hear the end of it. Casually, a man without a care, he took his own peek out the window. Wynn was nowhere to be seen, thank God. Out of sight, out of mind.

He grunted, then dropped into his seat, sprawling out and rubbing the back of his neck.

"No comment, huh?" Mick asked.

"I don't know what you're talking about." Ignorance was a lame defense, but he was too tired to think of much else at the moment.

Mick leaned forward over the table and whispered, "Possessiveness."

Josh turned. "She went in just a few seconds ago." He took his own seat. "Did you see the legs on that woman?"

"Since they're a mile long," Mick said, "they'd be a little hard to miss."

Josh lifted a brow. "She's put together right, I'll say that for her."

"You didn't have to put up with her first thing this morning." Wishing he could bite off his tongue, Zack took a long cooling drink of his cola.

Saluting him with his glass, Josh said, "She can get me up anytime."

"Ha ha." Mick shook his head at the double entendre, but amusement shone clear on his face as he looked between the two of them. "You have a one-track mind, Josh."

"And it's definitely on track right now."

Zack growled before he caught himself. "I hate to curtail whatever fantasy you're indulging, but she's off limits."

Josh hesitated with his drink almost to his mouth. "Says who?"

"Says me. I have to live by her. I'll be damned if you're going to date her, dump her, then leave her to me to deal with." Zack shook his head in adamant finality. "No way, so forget it."

Mick nudged Josh with his foot. "Besides, he's got his own plans."

Zack did bite his tongue this time. The more he said, the more they'd read into it, so denials would do him no good.

Eyeing Zack, Josh asked, "Is that right?"

"No, it is not right." He hoped like hell he sounded more definite than he felt. "Now can we talk about something else?"

"Because I can back off if you're making a personal claim."

Through his teeth, Zack said, "I'm *not* making a personal claim, but you *will* back off."

Josh stared at him a moment, then chuckled and switched his gaze to Mick. "I think you're right."

"Are we going to play cards or sit here mooning over women?" Zack barked.

"All right, all right," Josh soothed. "Don't get all fired up. We don't have to moon."

"Speak for yourself," Mick grumbled. "I'm mooning. I'd much rather be home with Delilah right now."

Josh shook his head in pity. Even Zack managed a credible chuckle. "You're still a newlywed, so you're allowed."

"And," Josh added, "Delilah is enough to make anyone moon."

Predictably, Mick bristled. Why in hell Josh continued to make those types of comments, Zack couldn't figure out. He knew there was a time when Josh had fancied himself taken with Delilah, too, but since she'd married Mick—an event Josh had supported wholeheartedly—Josh had roamed from woman to woman with a near insatiable appetite.

Mick half came out of his chair. "I wish you wouldn't speak so intimately about my wife."

Josh looked supremely unaffected by Mick's ire. "I was only agreeing with you."

"*You*—"

"Sheesh, men in love are so touchy," Josh complained. "First Zack breathing fire on me, and now you. A single man can't make a legitimate observation any more."

"Zack isn't married, *I am*."

"Zack wants to be married," Josh pointed out. "It's almost the same thing." Then he redirected his comments to Zack. "Is that it with Wynn? You considering her suitable wifely material?"

"No."

"Did you really see her backside?"

"No."

Josh grinned. "I'll take that first 'no' at face value. No way in hell am I accepting the second without some kind of explanation."

If he knew it wouldn't wake Dani, Zack would consider knocking Josh off his chair. Resigned, he gave up with a sigh. "She was bent over..." He faltered, unsure how to explain.

Josh protested his hesitation by saying, "I'm all ears."

"Actually," Mick admitted, "so am I."

"She had on short shorts—"

"I noticed that."

"So did I."

"Do you two *want* to hear this or not?" Zack glared at them both, waiting, but they now held themselves silent. "She was bent way over trying to drag a box into the backyard and her shorts rode up. That's all there is to it. I didn't see her whole behind." But he'd seen enough to know her backside was as delectable as her legs.

"A half moon, huh?" Josh made a tsking sound. "And here I missed it."

Zack gave up and explained in full the extent of his association with Ms. Wynn Lane. He told them about her family who'd soon be moving in, her brother who was built like a chimney, and her penchant for being outspoken and brazen and pushy.

"She is not," Zack reiterated, "wife material."

Josh had listened quietly, but now he waved away Zack's disclaimer. "Why do you want to get married anyway? I mean, just because Mick here found the perfect woman—"

Mick growled.

"—and *he's* blissfully happy, doesn't mean we all need to stick our necks into the noose. I know a lot more divorced couples than I do happily married ones."

Now that the cannon had been redirected, Zack relaxed and began shuffling the cards. "Dani asked me about feminine napkins the other day."

Both Mick and Josh froze, then gave near identical groans of emotional pain. "Commercials?" Josh asked.

"Yeah. She was watching cartoons when *bam*, there was a commercial for napkins. Can you believe it? She wanted to know what they were for and why women who used them got to go horseback riding and climbing and stuff."

Chuckling, Mick shook his head. "I can just imagine this conversation."

"Whatd'cha tell her?" Josh asked with interest.

"I fumbled my way through it." Actually, he'd made a total mess of things, but Zack wasn't about to admit that. "She wasn't ready to hear about the whole reproductive cycle thing—"

"Neither am I," Josh joked.

"—so I just told her women used them like they used perfume and makeup and panty hose."

Mick snickered. "Let me guess. She wants some."

"Yup. So you see, this is why I need a wife. I foresee stuff like this coming up all the damn time. I mean, what the hell will I know about fashion trends for teenage girls, or buying training bras?"

Josh considered that a moment, then said, "I could handle it if you want help. I wouldn't mind."

"Oh God, that's all I need! I can see the headlines now, Womanizer Extraordinaire Attempts Parenting 101."

"A female is a female is a female."

Mick tapped his fingers on the table. "Delilah would have something to say about that sentiment."

Josh grinned. "I know. She loves to give me hell."

"Girls start this puberty stuff earlier than guys, as early as eleven or twelve," Zack pointed out. He was amused despite himself, at the picture of Josh sorting through adolescent underwear. It was a far cry from lingerie, which admittedly, Josh knew a lot about. He bought enough of it for his girlfriends.

"I could handle it." Josh looked thoughtful, then grinned. "Hell, it might even be fun. I do enjoy shopping you know."

Zack did know. Every Christmas and every birthday, Josh took Dani shopping. They'd make a whole day of it, and Josh would spoil her with gifts and a movie and the amusement park. It was surprising, given Josh presented the world with only his preference for bachelorhood, yet Zack trusted him completely with his daughter.

In many ways, both Josh and Mick were pseudodaddies, picking up the slack whenever Zack ran short on time. And they did a great job. They'd helped him get through the loss of his wife, and helped even more in the transition from grief to thankfulness, because despite losing his wife, he still had Dani, and that was a lot, more than he'd ever asked of life.

Zack had inadvertently wandered down a maudlin path, so he changed the subject while dealing out the cards. "Mick, did Josh tell you his station is making a charity calendar?"

"What's this?" Mick asked.

Josh picked up his hand, rearranged the cards a few times, then said, "Some pushy promotions broad is organizing the whole thing. She wants a bunch of the men to pose in some cheesy way to go on the calendar, then they'll sell it and the proceeds will benefit the burn center."

"Pushy promotions broad," Mick repeated slowly, as

if savoring the words. "Does this mean she had the audacity to exclude you from modeling?"

"I never gave her the chance. Anyone who was interested was supposed to call her to set up an appointment." He peered over his cards at Mick and Zack. "To get ogled, no doubt. Can you believe that?"

Frowning, Zack asked, "Have you met her?"

"I don't need to. I heard all about her from a friend at a different station. She a rich daddy's girl who plays at this charity stuff out of boredom."

Mick and Zack shared a look. Mick laid his cards facedown and crossed his arms on the table. "Since when do you care about a woman's character?"

"Yeah," Zack said. "I thought it was the size of her bra cups that attracted you."

Josh suddenly looked harassed and annoyed, not that Zack minded after what he'd just been through. About time someone else took a turn on the hot seat.

"She's supposedly really beautiful, okay? And I've had it with women like that. I want someone more like Delilah."

Mick choked and his face turned red.

"Oh for God's sake." Josh quickly got out of Mick's reach and explained, "I wasn't—not for a second—saying Delilah's not beautiful! She is. Flat-out gorgeous."

Mick stood, looking far from placated.

"But she doesn't go in for all the props. When was the last time Del painted her nails or colored her hair? Never, right? She's genuine. Well that's the type of woman I want." He waved a hand toward the window. "Wynn what's-her-name would do, too. I want a natural woman, not a glamour doll who thinks she can crook her little finger and a guy will come running."

Mick subsided, but he looked far from appeased.

Zack shook his head. "Mick, you're going to have to get a handle on these jealous tendencies of yours. You know Josh won't poach."

"As if it'd do him any good to try!"

Zack sighed, but it turned into a laugh. "I wasn't suggesting it would. And seeing as you know that, why do you let his every comment rile you? You know he doesn't mean anything by it. It's just how he is."

Mick grumbled, "That wasn't your sentiment when he was trying to seduce Wynn."

It was Josh's turn to choke. "I wasn't trying to seduce the woman! Hell, all I did was hold her hand."

"You're both nuts," Zack concluded out loud. "Let's forget Wynn and the calendar and women in general. Mick, you can go on pining for your wife since I know you can't help it." He grinned. "Now, let's play cards."

Three hours later Zack was ready to call it a night. His neck was still stiff and his mind refused to pay attention to his hand, so he'd lost more than he'd won. Mick, too, was yawning, and mumbling that Delilah had likely finished writing for the night. Josh, the only one to look fresh, decided to call a woman from Zack's house and made plans to visit her that night.

Mick and Zack both shook their heads.

The night was cool and crisp and black as pitch when Zack waved goodbye from the doorway. He stood there until the headlights had disappeared out of the driveway, then he locked the door and tidied the kitchen.

On his way through the house, he picked up toys and drawings and a lone frilly sock peeking out from beneath a chair. He checked all the locks and headed upstairs.

Dani slept peacefully, her small body barely visible beneath the sheet. Zack smiled and pulled her door closed.

On his way to his own room he stripped off his shirt and stretched his aching arm and shoulder muscles. He kicked his shoes into the closet, then sat on the edge of the bed to remove his socks. After he turned out the light, he went to the window, breathing in the night air as he unzipped his slacks.

And from there, in a shaft of moonlight, reclining in the damn hammock like a sexual offering, he saw Wynn. For a single heartbeat lust raged through him, making his blood churn and his imagination grind.

Then a clearer picture formed; she looked to be sound asleep, which nearly made his mind explode with incredulity. She was a single woman, alone, in a new neighborhood, and she was stupid enough to pass out asleep outside, unprotected.

Jaw locked, Zack left his room with a stomping stride and iron determination. He'd known the moment he saw her that she was going to be nothing but trouble, both to his sanity and his libido.

5

THE WELL-TRIMMED GRASS was wet and slippery beneath his bare feet, and a gentle evening breeze stirred his hair. His temper remained hot; it rose in degrees as he closed in on her.

Wynn didn't so much as move an eyelash when he stood directly over her lush, limp body. She had one arm above her head, palm up, her fingers slightly curled. The other drooped over the side of the hammock, almost touching the ground. Those mile-long legs of hers were crossed at the ankle, her feet bare.

She'd changed clothes.

Zack surveyed her, at his leisure. Without those piercing hazel eyes watching him or her sharp tongue challenging him, he felt steady, more in control, free to look his fill.

The halter and shorts were gone, replaced by a long, loose white nightshirt that almost reached her knees. Or at least he thought it was a nightshirt—until he read the front. Lane's Gym—Workout For A Better Body. Obviously an advertisement for her brother's gym.

Clouds drifted across the moon, darkening the sky so that only the faint light from her porch illuminated her.

Her lashes looked feathery in the dark shadows, her mouth very, very soft.

The scent of shampoo and lotion rose from her warm body to mingle with the damp night scents.

Zack felt himself reacting to the sight of her, and it angered him. "Wynn."

She didn't move.

He didn't want to touch her. "Damn it, Wynn, wake up."

Her lashes stirred and a soft sound escaped her slightly parted lips, causing his abdomen to clench, his pulse to race. Then she resettled herself with a husky groan.

Zack's eyes flared. His stomach knotted with carnal awareness. He reached down and caught her shoulder for a brisk shake. "Damn it to hell, Wynn, will you get your ass awake before I—oompf!"

One moment he'd been indulging his temper and the next he found himself flat on his back in the dew-covered grass, the wind knocked out of him and Wynn's knee in his chest. Her fist was drawn back, ready to clout him.

Zack reacted as suddenly as she had, grabbing her legs and holding on as he flipped them both, putting her flat out beneath him. "What the hell is *wrong* with you?"

Both her knees came up to stove in his ribs and he groaned. Taking advantage, she pushed him facedown to the side and crowded in close to his back. Her elbow locked around his throat. He could hear her frantic breaths directly in his ear. "Just *what* did you think you were—"

Swallowing down a roar of anger, Zack reached back, caught her by the head, and flipped her over his shoulder. Her grunt was much louder than his and she wheezed, trying to catch her breath. She held still, not moving, just staring up as if to see if she'd broken anything.

Zack took immediate advantage, and this time when he covered her he did so completely. He held her wrists high over her head and pinned her legs with his, not about to risk his poor body again. Her knees had caught him so hard it felt like she'd broken his ribs. He'd always known her legs would be strong, but...

When she started to wiggle he squeezed her so tight she gasped. "What," he asked through his teeth, "the hell is the matter with you?"

He hadn't meant to yell, but never in his life had a woman attacked him physically. And absolutely *never* had he thought to attack a woman! Thank God there weren't many women like her.

When Wynn didn't answer, he leaned closer to try to see her face, now afraid that he'd hurt her.

She spoke barely above a whisper. "I didn't know it was you."

Zack grunted. So she'd thought she was defending herself? He was far from appeased. If she hadn't fallen asleep outside, it wouldn't have been an issue.

"Do you realize," she continued, "that I'm letting you do this?"

Disbelieving her gall, Zack reared back. "*Letting* me?"

Her head moved in a slight nod. "I could have bitten your face just seconds ago. Even your jugular."

"Of all the—"

"Even now," she taunted, "if I wasn't afraid of hurting you, I could toss you."

In that instant Zack became aware of her long lean body beneath him, the cushion of her plump breasts, the giving dip of her wide pelvis, the strong, sleek thighs... He had hold of her wrists—not delicate wrists, but large-boned for a woman—and he lifted them above her head, keeping her in a submissive position.

So he could control her.

Oh yeah, his body liked that a lot. Too damn much. He had no doubt she'd already noticed his hard-on, being as it was pressed rigidly into her soft abdomen. Well too bad. Zack leaned closer again so he could see her face. He looked at her lush mouth, open now as she struggled for breath, and then to her incredible hazel eyes. Damn she had sexy eyes. In nothing more than scant moonlight, they were the eyes of a wolf, and they stirred him. "Try it," he offered, and waited with his own breath held.

"Oh, no." She stared at his mouth, and he felt her attention like a hot lick. "I don't want to hurt you—now that I know it's you."

Without meaning to, Zack pressed into her. Only the thin cotton of her nightshirt and his slacks separated them from entry. He closed his eyes, tipped his head back and moved against her rhythmically.

The alignment of their bodies was perfect, chest to breasts, groin to groin. He could kiss her and ride her at the same time, and never miss a single deep stroke. That realization made his muscles ripple.

Her nipples had puckered and he felt them rasping against his bare chest. She shifted her thighs, maybe trying to accommodate him, but he refused to take any chances. Her arms hung limp in his grip, in no way fighting his hold. Still he secured her, stretching her out a bit more, aware of her strength, and her yielding.

He felt on fire. *"Wynn..."*

She lifted her head, as brazen as ever, and that was all it took. Zack had never been a man controlled by lust, never been a man to experience all that much lust.

But this...what else could it be called? Mere lust didn't seem adequate for the bombardment of sensations on his senses. He felt her everywhere, on his body, in his lungs, in his head and his heart.

She licked his mouth, making a sound of excitement and acceptance and hunger. He caught her tongue and drew it deep, then gave her his own. Their heavy breathing broke the quiet of the night, mingling with the faint sounds of crickets and rustling leaves. He switched both her wrists into one of his and brought his hand down to wedge between their bodies, cuddling her breast.

In reaction to his touch, her hips lifted so strongly she supported his weight off the ground for a suspended moment of time. It took one rough thrust for Zack to crush her down again.

He kissed his way to her throat and heard her ragged whisper. "Zack... Let me go."

"No." He thumbed her nipple, stroking, teasing.

A raw groan and a burst of movement later, Wynn had him on his back again. The woman was forever taking him by surprise. Zack almost wanted to laugh.

Until her thighs straddled his and she became the aggressor. Her hands opened wide over his bare chest, she stroked him and moaned with the pleasure of it. She nuzzled at his throat, then bit before licking and sucking and making him crazed.

The open vee of her thighs cradled his erection, and made him strain for more. He caught her behind in his hands, relishing the resilient feel of her, her softness in contrast with her feminine strength. He explored her, sliding his fingers over the silken material of her panties, pressing inward to touch her from behind. He found her panties damp, her body incredibly hot.

Cradling her hips, Zack urged her into a rough, slow roll that simulated sex and brought him dangerously close to the edge.

He was ready to take her, more than ready to get the ridiculous man's shirt off her body and touch her everywhere, kiss her everywhere.

Only he didn't have protection with him. And...

Reality dropped on his head like a ton of bricks. He actually groaned aloud with his disappointment, with the awareness of his responsibilities.

They were acquaintances of only a day, and not even a full day at that.

They were outdoors, in the open, and if he'd seen her through his bedroom window, his daughter could see them both if she should wake up and look out. Granted, that wasn't likely to happen, not the way Dani slept, but he didn't take chances with his daughter, not ever.

They were on the wet ground, mindlessly entwined and it was so unlike him, so unlike what he wanted for himself as a responsible father and server of the community, he felt appalled and embarrassed and rightfully angry.

At Wynn.

He caught her wrists again and held her hands still to enable him to gain control of himself. "Wynn."

His tone of voice had no effect on her. She wiggled free and attacked his mouth, kissing him so thoroughly he almost forgot his resolve. He turned his head aside. "No."

"Yes," she insisted. She grabbed his ears and held him still. Then, "God, you're incredible. So hard and sexy and sweet."

Sweet? Zack rolled to the side, literally dumping her off him, but the second she was flat, he stood. His chest worked like a bellows and his brain cramped at the effort it took to resist her. When he turned to look at her, his damn knees almost gave out. Her shirt had hiked up and he could see her panties, could even see her navel.

He stared—until she held out her arms to him and

the sight of her offering herself, wanting him, looked so good, so right, he couldn't stand it.

Jerking around, Zack said, "Get up."

He didn't watch to see if she did as he asked. He couldn't. Finally he heard a slight creak and turned to see her perched sideways on the hammock, her feet on the ground, her hands beside her hips, her gaze direct and waiting and unapologetic.

Zack drew a deep breath. "I'm sorry."

After a heavy beat of silence, she said, "Yeah, me too." She smirked and shook her head.

That drew him up. "Sorry for what?"

Wynn pushed to her feet and faced him eye to eye. "At the moment, I'm pretty sorry for everything." She turned away. "Good night, Zack."

He was so stunned by the dim sight of her wet back, the cotton shirt clinging to her behind and upper thighs, that he almost let her get away. He shook himself. "Wait a minute!"

"No point in waiting. Believe me, I understand."

Zack caught her arm and whirled her around. In the next instant she was on tiptoes and huffing in his face.

"Don't think for a single second that you bested me, buddy!" She poked him in the chest, making him stagger back a step. "The second I realized it was you, I went half-go. Besides that, you caught me asleep and sluggish. Now I'm wide awake and you're done kissing and you're acting all nasty and hateful again, so do *not* try manhandling me."

Zack had at least a dozen questions for her, but what

came out of his mouth was, "You actually think you could best me in strength?" He was so incredulous he barely knew what he said.

Wynn snorted. "I've trained all my life. I know exactly what I'm doing."

And she thought...what? That he was a marshmallow? She'd called him *sweet*. What the hell had she meant by that? Through his teeth, Zack heard himself say, "No way, lady. Not on your best day." Then he wanted to smack his own head for challenging a woman! *What was he thinking?*

With a look of utter disdain, she said, "You keep living that dream if it makes you happy, big boy." And again she turned to walk away.

"*Wynn.*" Even to his own ears, her name sounded like a warning. But then it had been strained through his clenched teeth.

Arms spread, she whipped around to face him and demanded, "*What?*"

He was a reasonable sort, Zack reminded himself. He was logical and calm and a pacifist. He absolutely, under no circumstances, wrestled with women, not even big bold pushy ones.

One slow deep breath helped a little. The second breath pushed the red haze out of his vision so he could see her clearly, or as clearly as the night-dark sky allowed. "Why," he asked, sounding more like a sane man, "were you sleeping on the hammock?"

She looked at the hammock as if to verify which one he meant. Then she shrugged. "I'd worked all day, I was hot and sweaty and after my shower I just wanted to rest my tired bones and get some fresh air. Only I nodded off. I didn't mean to fall asleep."

Zack clasped his hands behind his back to keep from reaching for her. Brows raised in inquiry, he said, "Do you, by any chance, know how risky that can be for a woman?"

"You mean with crazy neighbors lurking about ready to throw me on the ground and kiss me silly and paw me until I'm all excited and ready and then stop with no warning?" She gave him a smug, distinctly mean smile. "Yeah, I do now."

"I meant," he said, inching toward her, but watching her closely at the same time, "because of strangers who would do things to you without a second's hesitation. Men who would rape or murder or..."

"Rape and murder about covers it. No reason to go overboard."

"This is not a joke, damn it!"

She crossed her arms under her breasts and cocked one hip. It shouldn't have been a seductive pose, but damn, it made him sweat.

"Did I just say it was an accident, that I didn't mean to fall asleep? I thought I did, but given your attitude, I can't be sure."

Tension mounting, Zack flexed his shoulders and rolled his head on his neck. "It was irresponsible."

"Well, thank you, Mother, for your concern."

"Wynn, I know you're excited about your new house—"

"And my new neighbor? My new neighbor who likes to tease and lead women on, then pull away and act as if his finer sensibilities have been lacerated by my coarse and carnal behavior?"

Zack was again caught between wanting to shout with anger, and the urge to laugh. From the moment he'd met her, Wynn Lane had been too outspoken and honest for her, or his, own good. He rubbed his neck and concentrated on not smiling. "I didn't mean to tease."

"Oh? You call what you did—given the fact you pulled up short—fulfillment?" She shook her head. "You poor, poor man. You're missing the best part."

"Look, Wynn, it was a mistake for us to do—" He gestured at the ground. "—this. I don't know about you, but I'm not in the habit of indulging in one-night flings."

She didn't confirm or deny what her habits were, which only made him edgier. Little by little his neck and shoulder muscles tightened into a painful cramp. He'd strained something at work the night before, and arguing with Wynn only exasperated things.

Her eyes narrowed and she strode toward him. "What's the matter with you? Did I hurt you?"

His hand fell away from his neck. "Of course not."

"Ha! You're in pain, I can tell."

He started to say *she* was the pain, but held it in. It was past time he listened to himself. They were neighbors, no refuting that fact. They needed to get along in some civil but distant and detached way.

With that decision made, he waited until she stopped directly in front of him, then explained, "I dealt with two pretty nasty emergencies last night. The first was a case of domestic violence." His tone sounded raw even to his own ears, but the emotional devastation of the night still lingered. "I took a woman in with two broken ribs and multiple contusions. The bastard who'd worked her over had gone to a bar. Luckily the cops caught up to him there."

Zack had to be grateful that the man had been gone when he got there. He wasn't at all certain he could have contained himself otherwise.

Wynn, evidently sensing his turbulent emotions, reached out and smoothed her hand over his arm. It was a soothing touch, and it helped him to recall himself.

He shook off his lingering anger and reminded himself that the woman had pressed charges. That wasn't always the case, but luckily this particular woman had had enough. He'd left her in the hands of the social services.

"Then there was a car wreck. We had to cut the door away to get to the woman inside. She was in shock, covered in blood from a head wound, and getting her out wasn't easy, especially since she wasn't exactly a small woman."

"She was big like me?"

Zack's temper jumped a notch. "I could handle you easily without straining a thing."

She smirked.

"No, this woman was obese." Wynn remained quiet and waiting so he continued. "The reach was awkward, and I strained something in my neck and shoulders when I lifted her out."

"Hmmm. Sounds like you strained a trap. That happens a lot in clumsy lifts. Turn around."

He stalled. "What?"

"Trapezius muscle," she explained.

And Zack said, "I know what it is. I just didn't..."

Grabbing his upper arm, she forcibly turned him—something he allowed—and then began pressing her fingers into his neck, his shoulders, his spine. Zack groaned. Her touch had an electrifying effect that both soothed and excited.

"Right there?" she asked, her thumbs now working some hidden muscle that reacted by going limp.

"Yeah." And then, "You're good at this."

"I'm good at a lot of things."

His eyes shot open.

"Have you been using any moist heat?"

God, everything she said sounded sexual to his beleaguered brain. *Moist. Heat.* He was such a goner. "No," he croaked. "I haven't had a chance."

"Bull. You're a paramedic, you know better than to ignore injuries. If need be, you make time. Maybe instead of hanging out with your friends you should have soaked in your hot tub."

His brain took a leap from her suggestion, to a vivid fantasy of them both in the hot tub, steam rising and flesh wet... "I will later."

"When is later?"

Her persistence annoyed him. "Maybe after work to-morrow."

Her hands continued to massage and work his aching muscles. He felt like butter—like *aroused* butter.

"What hours do you work?"

That, at least, was a safe enough topic. "We're all on a rotating schedule. Ten hour days, four days a week. My hours are usually eight to six. The three days off vary and are almost never grouped together, but at least that way everyone gets a weekend now and then. And there's always overtime, so my hours end up fifty or over more often than not."

Leaning around to see his face, Wynn asked, "Who watches Dani while you work?"

"There's a lady two blocks down, Eloise. She's a real sweetheart, in her early seventies, on a fixed income. Dani adores her, and vice versa. Dani thinks of it as her second home."

"Any friends her own age?"

He shrugged. "She goes to preschool two days a week, but Dani tells me most of the kids there are 'babies.'"

Wynn chuckled. "Yeah, I can see her thinking that. She's used to adult company, isn't she?"

"Too much so. I thought the preschool would help, and she does enjoy it. One of her classmates lives in the neighborhood and she's had Dani over for birthday parties and special outings and things like that."

"Mmm. Sounds like fun for her." Hands splayed

wide, Wynn worked her way down Zack's back, over his lats, then his obliques. It was all he could do to remain standing.

Zack didn't mean to, but he felt so relaxed, so boneless from her massage, he heard himself confiding before he could censor himself. "She has a hard time fitting in with other girls."

"Oh?"

Zack closed his eyes, but now he had no choice except to explain. "She's...not into the same things as other little girls her age. The whole idea of playing dress-up revolts her, and she's outraged by the idea of frilly dresses and tights." He grinned, remembering the last time Dani had worn a dress. It had been for Mick and Del's wedding, and she'd only agreed because Del had helped her pick it out, and Del wasn't into lace and frills, either.

"I was the same when I was a little girl," Wynn said.

Zack teased, "You mean you were little once?"

Her thumbs pressed deep enough to make him jerk in pain. "Hey, ouch! All right, I was just teasing."

"I wasn't born an oaf, you know."

For the briefest moment Zack wondered if he'd hurt her feelings, then decided the massage must have softened his brain as well as his muscles. Wynn wasn't the type of woman who indulged fragile feelings.

On the tail of that realization came another, more startling one. Good God, was there a chance his daughter would grow up to be like Wynn? Wrestling in her yard, argumentative and loud and far too bold? The very idea made him shudder. He *had* to find a wife, a nice delicate feminine wife who adored Dani and could, with patience and a calm quiet demeanor, guide her into being a young lady.

"If you work fifty hours," Wynn said, breaking into his thoughts, "I imagine some of those nights it's pretty late when you get home."

"True."

"Do you bring Dani home?"

"Of course." He started to look at her, but she stilled him by working a particularly achy knot in his right deltoid. Damn, but she had wonderful fingers. "I was blessed with a real slughead for a daughter," he told her around a heartfelt groan. "It takes a lot to wake her before she's ready to wake. I just bundle her up and bring her home and tuck her into her own bed."

"If Eloise is in her seventies, how much longer do you think she can continue to baby-sit?"

"I've considered that," he murmured, his reserve now as limp as his muscles. "I'm thinking of leaving fieldwork."

"Yeah? To do what?" Her fingers found just the right amount of pressure, and he groaned low before he could work up the energy to answer. "Maybe be a supervisor," he said, "or an operations manager. Or maybe I'll instruct. I think I'd like that."

Wynn made a sound of interest, and her hands moved lower, over his gluteus medius, then his gluteus maximus...

Damn, but her fingers were magic...marvelous...
intimate!

Zack jerked around to face her. "You're seducing
me!"

She tried for an innocent expression and failed.
"Naw, just copping a feel of your nice tight buns."

He sputtered, both outraged and stupidly compli-
mented, and, if he was honest, vaguely turned on.
Okay, more than vaguely. He felt mellow and ready.
Primed even.

She had the gall to laugh in his face, then pat his
chest. "Relax Zack, your virtue is safe with me. And
you do feel better now, right?"

He flexed, rolled his shoulders in experimentation;
she was right, damn her. He gave a reluctant nod.

"Good." She patted him again, this time ending with
a caress of his pecs. "If you tighten up again, come see
me."

He was tight already, just not where she meant.

"It probably wouldn't hurt to use a little ultrasound
on the affected muscles, and I can do that at the gym."

"I'll be fine," he croaked.

She rolled her eyes. "You're a regular superhero,
aren't you? Impervious to the needs of your body, both
sexual and physical?"

Being pushy probably came naturally to her. She'd
likely been born making demands and causing con-
flicts. "I'm trying to do what's right for both of us and
you know it. We're neighbors. Anything beyond a
friendly association would be too difficult."

She gave a heavy sigh, saying, "Whatever," and turned to leave.

"I hope you understand," Zack called out, watching her as she walked into the light from her back porch. His body felt relaxed but zinging with life, too. An odd mix. A *carnal* mix.

She sent him an airy wave without looking back. A second later she went through the door and it closed with a click that echoed around the empty yards.

Damn irritating woman.

He'd made the right decision, despite his still raging hard-on. But then why did he feel so pissed off with himself? Why did he hate the right decision?

An upstairs light came on in her house, and through an open window Zack heard her begin to whistle again. She was a woman without a care, while he still stood there in the yard churning with a riot of emotions and physical needs. He stared at her window hard, willing her to move into view, but then the light went out and he knew she had gone to bed.

From now on, he'd just have to be very careful to avoid her. Given his hours, that's shouldn't be too hard to do.

WYNN WATCHED through her dark bedroom window as Zack tipped back his head and stared up at the moon. He looked so rigid, every line of his body denoting frustration, that she half expected him to howl, but all he did was turn on his heel and head back to his own house.

Her massage had been a waste, she could see that now; the man was determined to be tense. She sighed.

What a twist of fate, she thought, her heart sinking a little at the sight of his retreating back. Her hands were still tingling from touching him, from feeling all those smooth hard muscles and hot skin and vibrating tension. She huffed. The first man who really pushed her buttons, who made her feel like gelatin on the inside and made her breathe too fast just being near, and he was a blasted prude.

Her thought process crashed there and she was forced to face the possibility that he wasn't a prude at all. A man as big and sexy and intelligent and responsible as Zack was more likely suffering disinterest than moral restrictions.

Why would he be interested in *her*?

She'd done nothing but make a fool of herself since meeting him, and her naturally forceful personality had been in rare, suffocating form. But he brought out the extremes in her, and half the time she didn't even know what she was going to do until she did it.

She closed her eyes on a wave of remorse and embarrassment. God, she'd accosted him at every turn, provoked him and even rolled on the grass with him. She'd called him names and insulted him, and here she was, wishing he'd want her just a little?

Wynn shook her head. She was a complete and utter dolt.

She left the window and moved blindly toward the hall. She needed another shower—this one preferably ice-cold to chase away the lingering hunger. She knew she wouldn't sleep tonight, not after feeling him atop her, not after inhaling his aroused scent.

She had to get herself together, and she had to give the man some space. Rushing him was not the best tactic. No, Zack was a subtle man, when he wasn't challenging her. He was a father, and his sensitivity toward his daughter only made him more attractive. He was the hero Dani had described him as being, and by far the most appealing male Wynn had ever met.

Zack needed time to get used to her, to get to know her.

She'd *ease* her way in, she'd be charming and sweet and polite...because knocking down his defenses sure didn't seem to be working.

6

ZACK SAW HER every damn day. He woke up in the morning and she was outside working in the yard or cleaning her driveway or chatting with the other neighbors.

He got home from work and she'd just be coming in or going out.

He ran into her at the grocery store and once while they were both taking out their garbage. Dani chatted her up every time, like she was a long-lost and valuable friend. And Wynn was forever sweet and attentive—to Dani.

It irked him, especially since she lounged in that hammock every damn night. Before bed, he'd find himself standing at his window, watching for her like a lost soul. And sure enough, she'd come traipsing out, her long legs bare and her stride sure to the point of being almost mannish. Not that anyone would ever mistake Wynn Lane for a man. She was too curvy, too soft and...she smelled too good to be male.

His whole body would go taut watching her as she relaxed back in that hammock and stretched out the length of her sexy body. Damn if he didn't get aroused every time.

Sometimes she read until the sun went down. Sometimes she just swayed, music feeding into her ears through a set of headphones. She sometimes dozed and she sometimes whistled, but not once had she fallen into a sound sleep again.

He almost wished she would, so he'd have a legitimate excuse to seek her out, to touch her.

She no longer intruded. In fact, she seemed to have lost interest in him. Always she'd be cordial, give a wave or a friendly hello, and then she'd move on. She treated him the same as she did the other neighbors, and he didn't like it.

He'd never known himself to be such a fickle bastard before. But he missed her. He barely knew her and already he'd grown accustomed to her.

As had Dani.

Even now his daughter sat on the kitchen door stoop, wistfully staring at Wynn's house, waiting for her to appear. Dani missed her. She wasn't at all appeased by the short friendly chats or casual waves, and that wasn't something Zack had counted on.

It tore his heart out.

"Dani," he called, "come on in and eat your sandwich."

Two seconds later Dani peered in the door. "I'm gonna eat it out here."

Normally Zack would have been fine with that, but he didn't want his daughter turning melancholy. "Dani..."

"Wynn'll need a sandwich, too."

Zack went still and a strange emotion, one he refused to study too closely, swirled through him. "Is she out there?"

"She's with a bunch of big men."

Before his brain and feet could make a connection, Zack found himself at the door looking out. Sure enough, there was Wynn, surrounded by bodybuilders—three of them. All massive, all handsome.

All fawning over her.

He scowled, thinking to duck back inside before she or her cursed boyfriends spotted him.

His traitorous daughter did him in once again.

Dani took two bounding steps down the stoop to the lawn and waved her arms like a windmill. "*Hey Wynn!*"

Wynn looked up and her seven-watt smile shone brightly. She patted one of the guys on the chest, swatted at another's immense back and started in Dani's direction. Zack couldn't deny the pounding of his heart. It had been a week since he'd really talked to her, really been close to her. Deny it all he liked, he'd missed her. Maybe even more than his daughter had.

Dani shocked him by rushing to Wynn for a hug.

Wynn didn't shock him a bit when she bent down and scooped Dani high, tossing her in the air and then hugging her close. "What have you been up to munchkin?"

"You can eat peanut butter and jelly with me!"

Wynn glanced at Zack, saw the paper plate with the neatly sliced sandwich that he held in his hand, and said, "I *love* peanut butter and jelly. You don't mind sharing?"

"Nope."

When Wynn sat Dani down, she took her hand and stood staring at Zack. He cleared his throat. "How've you been, Wynn?"

"Busy. My folks are moving in tomorrow. I had to get everything put away and organized so they'd have a place to store their stuff. This moving on top of my moving is exhausting."

She snagged the sandwich, handed half to Dani and took a big bite of the other half. "Mmmm. Delicious."

Zack ignored that to ask, "Who are your guests?"

She gave a negligent shrug. "Guys from the gym. They wanted to see my new house and visit. They're also going to help me set up my patio furniture. I bought a picnic table with an umbrella and a glider and chairs and tables. I've got some plants, too. I can't wait to see it all together. The delivery truck should be here soon."

"It takes three giants to set up lawn furniture?"

Her eyes sparkled at the acrimony in his tone. Hell, he'd sounded almost...jealous.

Enunciating each word carefully she said, "They wanted to see my new house, too." Then she added, "You do have a problem listening to me, don't you? Or rather, you only hear certain selective parts."

Dani said, "I'll help, too."

"I dunno." Wynn pretended to study her. "I need strong laborers. Let's see your muscle."

Dani immediately flexed her skinny arm. She tucked in her chin and puffed out her cheeks and ground her teeth, with no visible effect.

Still, Wynn made approving sounds and squeezed the non-existent muscle. "Wow. All right, I think you're strong enough." She glanced at Zack. "That is, if your dad doesn't mind."

"He don't mind."

"Dani." She had jelly on her upper lip and a pleading look in her big blue eyes. He meant to reprimand her further, but she looked so cute...

"Please," Dani begged in her most hopeful tone.

Wynn chuckled at her theatrics, then leaned toward Zack, her hands clasped together now that she'd finished her half of the sandwich. Mimicking his daughter to a tee, she pleaded. "Pretty please, Zack. C'mon. We'll be careful. And I promise to watch her real close."

Zack eyed Wynn. She wore a baggy gray T-shirt today with denim cutoffs. She was barefoot, her frizzy flyaway hair in a ponytail on the very top of her head resembling a frazzled water fountain.

In a different way, a funny way, she was the most appealing woman he'd ever seen.

He gave up without a grumble and denied, even to himself, that he was using his daughter's wishes as an excuse. Dani wanted to be with her, so he'd allow it. But as her father it was necessary that he be there. That sounded plenty logical to him. "All right. But I'll help, too."

Wynn drew back. "You don't have to do that."

"I go where my daughter goes," he told her, letting her assume he didn't entirely trust her or her friends. She scowled in reaction, narrowing her beautiful eyes until they glittered golden with ire. He just grinned at her. Provoking her was way too easy.

"Fine." Then she said, "But you have to pass the muscle test, too."

"Don't be ridiculous."

"Hey, you're the one insisting. And fair's fair. Dani took the test."

Dani bounced. "Show her your muscles, Dad!"

"Yeah, show me, Dad," Wynn prodded, and Zack had the horrible suspicion that his neck had turned red.

Through his teeth, he said, "I promise, I'm strong enough."

Wynn shook her head. "Not good enough. I can see the muscles on my friends, and Dani proved herself." Her eyebrows lifted and her smile turned smug. "Now show me your stuff."

Zack knew he was in good shape. He had to attend daily workouts as part of his regimen for the station. He ate healthy food and his job was demanding, both mentally and physically.

But he wasn't in the habit of flaunting himself.

Wynn shoved his short sleeve up over his shoulder and said softly, "I promise this won't hurt a bit." She caught his wrist, locked her eyes with his, bent his arm at the elbow, and said, "Now *flex*."

Tightening his jaw in annoyance, Zack dutifully flexed. His biceps bulged. His arms weren't enormous like the body builders', but still plenty defined and impressive if he did say so himself.

Wynn's gaze softened and her eyes darkened. The hand holding his trembled. "Nice," she murmured in a voice that was far too intimate. "You just might do."

Dani went on tiptoe to point at Zack's upper arm. "There's where Dad got shot."

"*Shot?*"

Wynn started to look more closely, but Zack pulled away and jerked down his sleeve.

In that instant the delivery truck arrived and began backing into Wynn's driveway. After a long look at Zack, which promised the topic was far from finished, she turned to face the men who were milling around her yard. They appeared to be checking out every blade of grass and especially the hammock. To Zack, they looked like concrete blocks with legs.

"The truck is here," Wynn called out to them. "The payment is in on my hall table. Will one of you go grab it and sign for the stuff? I'll be there in just a minute."

Almost as an entity, they nodded agreement and began a pilgrimage to the front of the house. Wynn turned back to Zack. "Is there a swallow of milk to go with the sandwich? I swear that peanut butter is hung up right about here." She pointed between her breasts, well hidden beneath the gray cotton shirt, but Zack still went mute.

Luckily, his daughter played the perfect hostess. "We always have milk. Come on." She took Wynn's hand and led her into the kitchen. Zack was forced to follow.

"You need to regulate your eating habits better," he grumbled.

She slanted him a look as he took a tall glass from the cabinet. "Do I look malnourished? Vitamin deficient?"

Since she was tall and strong and healthy, Zack ignored that question. He filled the glass to the top and handed it to her. "And I can't believe you're letting those men sign for your belongings. Or go through your house unchaperoned."

She'd already guzzled down half the milk when his words registered. With the glass tilted to her mouth, her gaze captured his and she blinked. Very slowly she lowered the empty glass and set it aside. She licked her lips. Two seconds passed before she said, "Marc and Clint and Bo are good friends. And they can be trusted."

Dani hovered near the door, watching the men. "They sure are big."

With an evil smile, Zack said, "Wynn evidently likes them that way."

Her smile was no less taunting as she leaned close and breathed into his ear, "But I wasn't in my backyard, on the ground, making out with any of *them.* Ever." Then she straightened and asked, "How'd you get shot?"

"By bein' a hero," Dani said, still with her head out the door.

Wynn turned to Zack. "Gunfire?"

How she managed to pack so much horror into one small word was beyond him. She acted as though the idea was ludicrous, as if he wasn't man enough... Deciding to nip that thought, and this conversation in the bud, Zack grabbed her arm and put his hand on his daughter's narrow back, urging them both forward. "If we're going to help we better get to it. No more time for gabbing."

Dani skipped ahead. "What should I do?"

"I have some new baby plants that need extra special care until I get them in the ground," Wynn told her. "You can move them from the back porch under the overhang to the yard so the men can set up the furniture without trampling them. I trust you more than I do all these big lugs."

Dani took off like a shot and Zack yelled, "Be very careful, Dani, and don't get in anyone's way."

Dani was no sooner out of hearing when Wynn asked again, "How'd you get shot?"

"It's nothing."

"Ohhh," she cooed in a dramatic voice, "I just love a humble martyr." She batted her eyes at him, laughed, then said, "No really. What happened?"

"You are such a pushy woman."

She stopped, which caused him to stop since he still had hold of her arm. Realizing that, he let her go and propped his fists on his hips.

"What?" he asked, when she continued to look at him.

For the first time that he could remember, she actually looked sheepish. "I didn't mean to be pushy," she muttered, and her face heated. She didn't blush well,

Zack decided, seeing her entire face, neck and even her ears turn pink.

"It's a...well, a bad habit I guess. Sorry." She started to say more, shook her head, and stepped around him. Zack caught her arm again.

"Wynn."

She stopped, but rather than face him she looked down at her feet.

Zack stared at the back of her head where frazzled strands stood out on end, having escaped the band she'd used to contain her hair. The curls resting against her nape actually looked kind of cute, maybe even a little sexy. She had an elegant neck and broad, sexy shoulders...

Suddenly Zack felt a searing scrutiny.

He looked up and caught all three of the hulks watching him. One man had a large wrought-iron chair held aloft in his arms, which he continued to hold with seemingly no effort though the thing looked awkward and heavy.

The other two had a cumbersome settee between them, with yet another chair balanced in the middle of it. They, too, seemed more than comfortable with their burden.

Zack tugged on Wynn's arm. "That's some massive furniture you bought."

She shrugged, still staring at her feet. "I'm a big girl. I need big furniture to be comfortable."

"True. Those are also big, apparently protective guys you've got hauling it."

Wynn caught his meaning and looked up. Whatever dejection she'd been feeling fell away to be replaced by her natural arrogance. "Oh, for goodness' sake. Are you three going to stand there all day?"

One of the men, an artificially tanned behemoth, smirked. "Only until we see that you're all right."

Sounding incredibly surprised, Wynn asked, "You're worried about *Zack*?" And to compound that insult, she hitched her thumb over her shoulder toward him, then chortled. "Don't be silly."

One of the men holding the settee bared his teeth in what might have been loosely termed a smile. "Only Wynn would call us silly," he said to Zack, then added, "I'm Bo. A...friend."

The other two grinned at that, which made Wynn bristle, and Zack scowl. Just what the hell did Bo mean? Was it an inside joke? Did Wynn and Bo have some sort of understanding? Were they involved?

The guy on the other end of the settee said, "Bo, Wynn is going to get you for that," and then to Zack, "I'm Clint and that over there is Marc."

Zack nodded. "I'm her neighbor, Zack Grange."

"Yeah right." They all chortled again, looking between Wynn and Zack. "Just a neighbor."

Zack clenched his teeth. "The little one running around is my daughter, Dani."

Bo winked. "She's a sweetheart. And hey, Wynn just loves kids."

Wynn cast a quick look at Zack, then under her breath said, "You guys are in for it."

They pretended great fear, gasping and sharing worried glances—ludicrous considering their impressive sizes. Growling, Wynn took a threatening step forward and they quickly dispersed, rushing to the patio to put the furniture down.

Zack pulled her around to face him. She looked braced for his anger, until he asked, "Is Bo a boyfriend?"

Her eyes widened and she choked on a laugh before saying, "No! Of course not."

"Then what was all that inside snickering and shared looks?"

She waved that away. "Bo flirts with all women, sort of like your friend Josh. He's got about a dozen girlfriends and yes, he pretends to want to add me to the list, but it's all just in fun. I'm not an idiot and he knows it."

That brought up another issue that nettled, and Zack said, "You acted plenty interested with Josh."

"Ha! He's gorgeous and he took me by surprise. I'm used to Bo being outrageous, but not other guys. That's all." She looked Zack over and asked, "What about you? Any steady girlfriends?"

"No." But not for lack of trying on his part. He just hadn't met a woman yet who was right for him and Dani, and he saw no reason to get involved in a *wrong* relationship.

Except that with Wynn...he was tempted.

She looked skeptical, but said only, "You don't have to worry about those three. They're just a little overprotective, but now that I've assured them you're harmless, they'll let it go."

"Harmless?" He stepped closer to her, until they almost bumped noses. "One of these days I'm going to make you eat all these insults."

Her eyes brightened and filled with fascination. "Is that right? How?"

"A number of ideas are zinging through my head."

In the vein of being helpful, she suggested, "We could wrestle again. Next time you *might* win."

Damned irritating, irrational... He let her go and stalked away. He heard her satisfied snicker before she suddenly went quiet, groaned, and then began tromping after him.

And here he'd actually thought he'd missed her. Ha! He couldn't be that stupid.

But he *was* smiling.

THE PATIO BEGAN to look just as Wynn had pictured it. She'd had the furniture rearranged three times, despite all the guys grumbling, but now everything worked. Including the beautiful new gas grill, which Zack had suggested she move away from the window, to keep smoke from coming into the house.

About half an hour ago at the hottest part of the afternoon, Zack had removed his shirt. His back and shoulders glistened with sweat, as did the straight, light-brown hair clinging to his nape and temples. His blue eyes looked even bluer in the bright sunshine, and the flex of his lean, athletic muscles made Wynn more aware of him than she'd ever been of any man.

She saw Zack lift his head and look around for Dani. He was good at doing that, at always being aware of his daughter and what she was up to. Wynn couldn't imagine a more attentive or caring parent.

Zack shaded his eyes until he located Dani sitting in the grass beneath a large tree. She was hunting for four-leaf clovers with Clint, who appeared suitably impressed with her skills while he drank an ice-cold cola.

Zack smiled, his face lit with so much love and pride, Wynn thought her heart might burst.

She needed to be with him again.

A week had gone by where she'd done her best to give him time and space, but she didn't think she could take it anymore.

Bo walked up and thwacked her on the behind. "I need sustenance after all my toils. You got any lunch meat?"

A quick peek at Zack showed his attention had shifted and he now had that scowling, disapproving look on his handsome face again. Resisting the urge to rub her stinging behind, Wynn huffed. It wasn't exactly her fault that her brother's friends were all too familiar. "I thought I'd order a pizza."

"No need, darlin'," Marc told her. "We can't stay that long. But a sandwich would hit the spot."

She flapped her hand toward the kitchen. "There's all kinds of lunch meat and fixings in the fridge. Go help yourself."

Bo thwacked her again, almost knocking her off her feet with the sharp swat. She was just irascible enough to give him a reciprocal punch to the shoulder, which he most likely didn't even feel despite his cringing facade of pain.

Clint called out, "Fix me one, too!" and Marc nodded as he went inside with Bo.

Wynn walked to the other end of the patio and dropped down into her settee. The forest-green and cream striped cushions were soft and plush and she smoothed her hand over them with deep satisfaction. This was hers, all of it, the house, the tree-shaded yard, the hammock and...her neighbor. All hers.

She caught Zack watching her and she smiled. "It looks good, doesn't it?"

Zack appeared to be so annoyed she wasn't at all sure he'd answer. Then he sat down beside her. "It's very nice. You have good taste."

As he spoke, he stared out at the yard toward his daughter, giving Wynn his profile. She sighed, knowing his thoughts when he hadn't shared them. "Bo is just...Bo. I've known him almost as long as I've known Conan. They went through school together and stuff. He really doesn't—"

"Show any hesitation at touching your behind? Yeah, I noticed. I also noticed that you don't seem to mind."

Her lips tightened as her temper rose. "He treats me like a kid sister most of the time."

"Uh-huh." Zack turned to face her, his expression set. "I don't know why I'm even surprised, considering..." He made a disgusted sound and turned away again.

Her heart thumped hard and her stomach roiled. "Considering what?" When he didn't answer, she said, "Zack, don't you dare be a hypocrite. I wasn't the only one out there that night. We both got carried away."

He ran a hand through his hair. "I've never in my life done anything like that, so it had to be because of you."

He said that so casually, casting the blame without hesitation, that she wanted to throttle him. "*You* snuck up on *me* that night!"

"I did not sneak," he grumbled.

"Ha! I was asleep."

"Yeah, and what woman does *that?*" He jerked around to face her, looking angry and befuddled and very much like an attentive male. "What woman sleeps out in her backyard at night, exposed?"

"I wasn't *exposed*, you ass. You make it sound like I was naked or something." She shook her head, realized she'd just insulted him again, and wanted to bite off her tongue. She drew a breath and tried to sound reasonable. "Zack, I was just—"

He didn't let her finish. "I don't get carried away like that. Ever."

To Wynn, he still looked accusing, and all she could think to say was, "You did that night."

His eyes narrowed, then his gaze flicked over her. "Yeah. Bad judgement on my part."

Wynn sucked in a breath. *Damn, that hurt.* She wasn't sure if she wanted to punch him or cry. She wasn't much of a crier and seldom indulged, but now she felt dangerously close to giving in to tears. Her bottom lip even quivered before she caught it between her teeth.

For a brief moment, Zack looked guilty. "Look, Wynn, it's really none of my business what you do."

"I want it to be your business," she admitted softly.

His spine stiffened—and Bo shoved a sandwich into his face. "I figured you had to be hungry, too."

Zack studied Wynn a second longer, then warily looked up at Bo. "Thanks."

"No problem. 'A friend of Wynn's,' and all that." Bo pursed his lips and continued to glare down at Zack. "You *are* a friend, right?"

Wynn quickly stood and placed herself between the two men. "Back off, Bo. I mean it."

In the next instant, she yelped as she found herself yanked back down onto the soft settee. Zack had grabbed the waistband of her shorts and literally jerked her off her feet. She sat gawking at him while he stood and met Bo eye to eye. Zack wasn't as bulky as the bodybuilders, but he was all lean hard muscle.

"Actually," Zack said, "I'm more of an acquaintance at this stage."

"A friendly acquaintance?"

"You got reason to think otherwise?"

The male posturing had Wynn on edge. She would definitely strangle Bo later, and what in the world was wrong with Zack? She thought him to be a sweet, considerate, passive man. Not one to indulge in games of male one-upmanship. Yet he'd brought on as much attitude as Bo, and that was saying a lot.

A new voice intruded, full of good humor and mocking concern. "Making yourself the center of attention again, Zack?"

Wynn twisted in her seat, and found herself almost face-to-belt buckle with Josh, who stood just at the end of the patio, right behind the settee. He wore tight faded jeans and a white T-shirt that read: Firefighters Take The Heat.

Zack, too, turned to face him. "What are you doing here?"

Josh smiled and leaned down, bracing his arms on the settee back, looming over Wynn. She wanted to scoot away, especially with the dark frowns Zack sent her way, but she was a bit too surprised to move.

"I came to let you know that lunch is cancelled for today," Josh said. "Mick insists on escorting Del to a coroner's for some research she's doing." He nodded at the sandwich still squeezed into Zack's hand. "But I see you'd forgotten all about our lunch."

Wynn lurched to her feet, feeling dreadful. "Ohmigosh. I interrupted your plans?" She looked between Josh who was smiling and Zack who was scowling. She ignored Bo.

Josh skirted the settee and again placed himself close to her. He even slipped his arm around her waist. She wasn't sure what to do. "Don't worry about it, Wynn. We meet nearly every week for lunch, so missing one now and then isn't a big deal."

Zack handed the sandwich to Wynn, who accepted it without thinking. Then he crossed his arms over his chest in a confident pose and said, "Josh, meet Wynn's erstwhile protectors. Bo and Marc and out there in the grass with Dani is Clint."

Bo and Marc nodded, but Clint was unaware of the additional guest. He was a grade school teacher with three daughters of his own and loved children in general. Wynn thought of him as a gentle giant, and smiled when she saw he was making Dani a flower garland out of clover buds.

Josh reached out to shake hands. He had his engaging grin in place, but his dark green eyes were alight with mischief. "Josh Marshall. How're you all doing?"

"They were just about to leave," Wynn said, trying for a not-so-subtle hint.

Bo just rolled his eyes. "Quit worrying, doll. We're not going to manhandle your neighbor."

Josh sputtered on a laugh. "Manhandle Zack? Of course not. You know he's a paramedic, right?"

Blank faces stared at Josh.

"Well he is, and paramedics have to stay in great shape. So, don't let him fool ya. I've seen Zack lift three-hundred pound men and carry them like they were infants. I've seen him work tirelessly through frozen snow for hours when cars piled up on the highway, and I've seen him go twenty-four hours without a single sign of exhaustion. He's got more dexterity and physical coordination than you can imagine, and he—"

Zack interrupted to say, "Can leap tall buildings in a

single bound? Is faster than a speeding bullet?" His tone was dry, his expression chagrined.

Josh laughed. "I don't know about jumping buildings, but I've seen the bullet wound on your arm, so no, you're not all *that* fast."

Wynn jumped on that verbal opportunity. "I've seen it, too. How did it happen, do you know?"

"Sure I know. I was there."

"Josh," Zack warned, but now that everyone had redirected their attention from animosity to curiosity—all but Zack who still looked plenty defensive—Wynn wasn't about to back down.

And neither was Josh. "We were called to the scene of a riot. Buildings burning, glass everywhere, people down in the street."

"Dear God," Wynn muttered, easily able to picture the chaos. She'd never thought of Zack being involved in something so violent, and now that she did, fear swamped her.

Josh nodded. "Innocent people were cowering in alleys, afraid to move, *unable* to move. A woman had caught a stray bullet in the chest and she was just lying on the ground right in the middle of the worst of it, literally bleeding to death. Police were everywhere, SWAT teams were on the way. But we were afraid she'd die before we could get to her."

Wynn already knew what Josh would tell her, and in that moment she felt herself tumbling head over heels in love. To hell with logic or time or background. Her heart knew all it needed to know; she sank down onto the settee with her very first case of weak knees.

Zack shook his head. "It wasn't nearly so dramatic. Plenty of officers provided cover for me."

"Not well enough," Josh pointed out. "You took that slug to the upper arm. Actually," Josh continued, "he got shot when he covered the woman with his own body, trying to protect her from getting hurt worse. No doubt her body couldn't have sustained another serious injury."

"It was all fine in the end," Zack grumbled, and he started looking around for his shirt.

"Yeah." Josh grinned. "As I recall she was so grateful to Zack after that. Really grateful, if you get my meaning."

Marc and Bo chuckled in male understanding. Wynn rolled her eyes.

Zack said, "Shut up, Josh."

"My lips are sealed."

Zack finally found his shirt and pulled it on. Wynn mourned the loss of seeing his sexy naked chest, and she really wanted to examine that scar from the bullet more closely. "Dani said you were a hero."

He grunted. "Dani is four years old and adores me, which is only right since I'm her father. Truth is I just do my job, the same as anybody else."

Josh, still pretending to have zipped his lips, hummed a reply to that.

"Oh, knock it off," Zack snapped. He took his sandwich back from Wynn and took a healthy bite.

Wynn shook herself. "Since I interrupted your lunch, Josh, can I make you a sandwich, too?"

Bo clutched his heart. "You're going to make him a sandwich? Hell, we're the ones who worked for you all afternoon and you didn't offer to serve us."

Wynn elbowed him hard. "All of you behave," she said, and she encompassed Zack in that order, before heading toward the patio door. She caught Josh's arm as she went and dragged him along with her. "We'll be right back."

7

WYNN GOT JOSH inside the door, pulled him around the corner and flattened him against the wall. "I'm so glad you dropped in."

Josh, looking startled, said, "Uh," and clasped her upper arms to keep her from getting any closer. "Yeah, see, I sorta thought...well..." He looked around and to Wynn, he appeared hunted.

It took her a second to figure out what bothered him, and then she laughed. Men could be such big frauds!

"Look, Wynn..." He inched her a little farther away from him, while keeping his own body plastered to the wall. "Do you think it's safe to leave them all alone out there? I sensed some hostilities going on when I arrived."

"That's why you started defending Zack?"

"Hey, he's a friend. Besides, it's true. He can take care of himself. You know that, right?"

She shrugged, then daringly pressed closer, just to watch him squirm.

"The thing is," he blurted, looking all around again as if he expected someone to jump him at any second, "I thought you had a thing for Zack."

Wynn smoothed her hand over his very solid, very large shoulder and whispered, "I do."

"Because I'm not at all sure—" He did a double take. "You do?"

"Mmm-hmm." She looked him in the eyes, licked her lips, and continued, "That's why I dragged you in here." She patted his cheek and added, "To find out more about Zack."

"Oh. *Oh!*" Josh laughed and his confidence returned in his quirky smile and the way his shoulders relaxed. "Good. That's real good. Just what I wanted to hear."

"But Zack doesn't like me much."

"I think he likes you *too* much. That's the problem, at least as far as he's concerned." She stepped back and together they headed toward the kitchen. "Personally, I think you're perfect for him."

Wynn had never in her life been described as perfect. Her father harped on and on about her imperfect hair, and her mother harped about her lack of femininity and her brother drove her crazy telling her she was too aggressive while constantly challenging her. It was a rather nice compliment to hear. "No kidding?"

"Hell yeah." He pulled out a chair for her. "Look at you! You're attractive and healthy—being a paramedic, and having lost his first wife, Zack is big on health."

Wynn blinked at that sentiment.

"You're also fun and funny and you seem to like Dani." He frowned. "That's a must you know, that you like his daughter. And you can't fake that because plenty of women have tried and he's always seen through them."

Wynn fell speechless at such a wealth of verbal outpourings. She hadn't had to ask a single question!

He looked a little worried at her continued silence. "You do like Dani, don't you?"

Unwilling to lose this golden opportunity, she gathered her wits. "Of course. She's adorable. Smart, precocious, bold." She shrugged. "Beautiful like her dad."

Josh grinned. "Zack is beautiful, huh? What a hoot."

Wynn realized exactly what she'd said and blushed. "Don't you dare say anything to him."

"Oh, no, no, of course not."

Wynn didn't believe him for a second. "Josh..."

"Do you really have something to eat?"

One thing about men, you could always count on them wanting food—especially the big ones. Josh obviously spent his fair share of time in the gym pumping iron. His physique and looks were so impressive, he could have posed for a centerfold. "Sure. Help yourself."

He laughed at that. "So your muscle-bound friends were right, huh? You don't cater to men?"

Actually, she'd been so preoccupied formulating all her questions, she'd forgotten all about her manners. "Sorry." She stood. "I've had a lot on my mind."

Josh immediately pressed her back into her seat and then patted her shoulder. "Hey, you've been working all day and I'm a big boy, I can feed myself. It was just an observation."

Propping her head on both hands, she groaned. "This is awful. It's been so long since I dated, or since I tried to attract a guy, I'm going about it all wrong."

She heard the cabinets open. "You trying to attract Zack?"

"Without much success."

"Not true." The refrigerator opened and Wynn watched through her fingers as Josh poured out a glass of juice and hauled out sandwich fixings. She'd have to remember to stock up on more lunch meat now that she had her own home and had such big men living nearby and visiting.

Taking his own seat, Josh said, "Zack has noticed you big time. He's just in denial."

"You think?"

"I know." He piled enough meat on his sandwich to make a meal. "Zack hasn't acted this upside down about a woman since his wife."

Wynn wondered how to broach that subject, then decided against trying to dredge up tact she didn't have. It was pointless. She said simply, "Will you tell me about her?"

Josh popped a whole slice of bologna into his mouth and nodded. "Young, beautiful. Very sweet and very petite." He eyed Wynn. "Nothing like you, expect maybe the beautiful part."

Heat rushed into her face. Josh was such an outrageous flatterer! She decided the best thing to do was ignore it. "I'm only twenty-eight. Not exactly old myself."

"Ancient compared to Rebecca."

So, Zack was attracted to young, petite women? Just what she didn't want to hear. "That was her name? Rebecca?"

"Yep. She would have turned twenty-one a month after having Dani if she hadn't died."

Very young. Though Wynn didn't know the woman, it hurt her to think of it. Dani and Zack had lost so much. She rubbed her forehead. "How long had they been married?"

"Only about seven months. The pregnancy was a surprise, and the reason for the marriage. Once Zack found out, he insisted, and Rebecca gave in. I'm not sure it's what either of them really wanted at the time."

Wynn did some math in her head and decided Zack was around twenty-five or so when he'd married, not much older than that when he became a father. Wynn swallowed hard. "How did she die?"

Josh laid the food aside and leaned back in his chair. He looked past Wynn, and he appeared more somber than she'd thought possible. "Rebecca had a hard time with the pregnancy. She was so small that it put a hell of a strain on her body. Her ankles swelled, her back hurt, her...well, you get the idea."

"Yes."

"She wasn't at all happy about the physical changes, so her emotional state of mind wasn't the best, either. She wanted Dani, no doubt about that, but she was pretty damn miserable those last few months. Physically and emotionally."

"I think that's pretty common, isn't it?"

Josh shrugged. "I suppose, what with hormone changes and all that." Then he shook his head. "Zack and I were both at a huge warehouse fire when she went into labor five weeks early. She called the station, and they immediately went to work on getting someone to replace Zack, but the destruction was huge and they were running short on manpower. Damn near everyone had already been called into service. Zack was working his ass off, dealing with a dozen different traumas, worried and anxious and madder than hell because he couldn't just leave. Leaving would have been a firing offense, though, which might not have stopped him except that he would never deliberately walk away from seriously injured people. And that's what he would have had to do. He thought Rebecca was okay, that she'd made it to the hospital and they were taking care of her..."

"But?"

Josh got up from the table. Like Zack's house, she had a window right over her sink, and that's where he went. He shoved his hands into his back pockets and stared out at the yard. "The contractions came too fast and she couldn't drive. She lost control of the car and it went off the road, flipping into a ditch. She took two other cars with her, but no one else was seriously hurt. By the time she was airlifted to the hospital, she'd died. They managed to save Dani."

Wynn nearly strangled on her own emotion. Her throat felt tight, her stomach ached and her heart beat painfully. She could only imagine what Zack had gone through.

"He's usually a rock," Josh said quietly. "Nothing rattles him. He's always calm and polite and reasonable. Always."

She looked up. *Zack* was calm and reasonable? Well, yes, he could be, she supposed. But he could also be forceful and outrageous and around her, he was seldom calm.

"That was the closest I've ever seen him come to losing it." Josh turned to face her. "That bullet wound he's got? Well, he knew he'd get shot when he went after that woman. I don't mean that he thought the odds would be good, I mean that he knew some of the rioters were firing *at* her, determined not to let her be saved, just to prove some fanatical point. Zack put himself between her and those bullets. He willingly risked his life for a person he didn't know from Adam. That's just how he is. He can't bear to see anyone hurt."

He drew a breath, then finished. "You can imagine what it did to him that he wasn't there for Rebecca."

"He blamed himself?"

"Yeah, he did. For a while. Then Dani got to him. For almost two weeks she was a perfect baby. Cooing when she was hungry, sleeping sound, and then bam, right out of the blue she became a tiny demon." Josh laughed. "Man, she put Zack through hell. He'd come in off a long shift and the sitter would say that Dani had slept and had been happy. Then she'd hear Zack and start making demands. When he was around, she wanted him to hold her. She wouldn't let him give her only half his attention."

Wynn considered all that. "You're saying he ignored her at first?"

"Hell, no. He made sure she was taken care of and he kissed her goodbye and hugged her hello, but he wasn't yet attached to her. He felt a responsibility for her, but he had so much grief, so much remorse, there wasn't much room for anything else, much less love. Till Dani took over."

"He's a good father."

"He's a *great* father. The absolute best. And he'd make a helluva husband, too."

Wynn was just digesting that not so subtle hint when Zack growled from the doorway, "I appreciate the accolades, Josh, but you're *way out of line.*"

Josh said, "Uh, you didn't leave any dead bodies outside, did you?"

"Knock it off." He walked farther into the room. "You know I'm a pacifist."

"Right. Whatever you say." He skirted around Zack with theatrical fanfare, and said, "I think I'll talk to your friends, Wynn. They seem like very nice fellows."

The screen door fell shut a second later. Wynn slowly came to her feet to face Zack. "Nice fellows," he mimicked. "They seemed like possessive, jealous fellows to me."

"Protective, not possessive. I told you I haven't dated any of them."

"Did you? I don't seem to recall that conversation."

She cleared her throat. "Everything okay outside?"

He advanced on her, his gaze locked on hers. "If you mean has everyone played nice, yes. But your bully boys gave me the third degree."

"They didn't!" Dismay filled her. How could she make a good impression on a man like Zack if Bo kept behaving like an ass?

"They did."

As he reached her, she stepped behind her chair. She wasn't afraid of Zack, but she didn't understand his mood either. He seemed on edge, yet also sort of...accepting. But accepting of what? Something was definitely different, of that she was certain. "I'm sorry."

"They seem to think you have your 'sights set on me,' as they put it."

Oh God, oh God, oh God... She just knew her face was flaming. She only had one brother, and he was enough to contend with without his friends trying to take over the role, too. Hoping to excuse their bizarre behavior, she said, "I, ah, don't show a lot of interest in the opposite sex."

Zack cocked a brow. "What are you telling me? *Males* don't interest you?"

"No! That is, I meant that I don't show a lot of interest in *any* sex."

One side of Zack's mouth curled in an amused, mocking smile.

She bit her tongue, then took two long breaths. "I *mean*," she stated, "that I don't usually chase a guy. I've got friends, and that's it." And so she didn't sound pathetic, she added, "That's as much as I want."

His voice was oddly gentle when he quipped, "Glad to hear it."

He was now so close she felt his breath when he spoke. Just two inches and she could be kissing him again. She considered it, but held back because she didn't know if he'd be receptive to the idea. So far he'd acted really put out over their mutual attraction—even to the point of denying it was mutual.

Which, she realized, meant he was so close because he wanted to intimidate her. She frowned. "That was before meeting you, Zack. I want you. I haven't made a secret of that. But you should understand that what happened in the yard the other day was an aberration for me, too. I don't regret it, but no way has it ever happened before."

His mouth twisted, and she got the awful suspicion he didn't believe her.

Wynn lost her temper. "Just because I have big male friends—"

He rolled his eyes.

"—and I got carried away with you—"

"We *both* got carried away."

She completely missed his confession in the middle of her tirade. "—doesn't give you the right to assume I'm free with all men."

"It also doesn't give you the right to go snooping around in my private business. If you wanted to know about my wife, you should have asked me."

Her chin lifted so she could look down her nose at him. "Would you have told me anything?"

"No." Before she could finish her full-fledged huff, he added, "Because it's none of your business."

Wynn threw up her hands. "There, you see? Talking to you is pointless!" She realized she wasn't helping her case any, but really, what could she do? She couldn't change herself; she wouldn't even know where to begin. She let out a sigh and dropped her head. "Actually," she muttered, "I guess all of this is pointless, huh?"

Zack drew himself up. "What does that mean?"

"It means I'm beginning to accept that you're one hundred percent not interested." She lifted her shoulder in a halfhearted shrug. "I did hear all about your wife, and I know now that you're more attracted to petite women." She even snorted at herself in self-disgust. "God, I'm so far from petite it's laughable."

"Wynn." He said her name like a scold.

She held out her arms. "I'm a great big lummox of a girl and I know it. I'm not cute or petite or any of those nice things. You like little weak women who you can protect, and I don't need protection. I'm not even weaker than you."

His expression bemused, he rumbled, "Uh, actually you are. A lot weaker, damn it."

But she barely listened to him now. She was too upset with the realization that Zack would likely never want to be involved with her. "I'm all wrong for you."

She paced around her kitchen, for the first time unmindful of the fine cherry cabinets and her new stainless steel sink and her side-by-side refrigerator, which just yesterday she'd kept touching because she loved it so much. Even the pleasure of getting her patio set up was now ruined.

Dejected, she turned to face him and said, "I'm sorry. I guess I've been a total pain in the butt."

"Yeah."

Though he said it gently, her shoulders slumped.

Then Zack stepped closer and he cupped her face carefully in his two hands and he said almost against her lips, "You are a pain in the neck, Wynn, and a pain in the ass and everywhere else. But you know why." And with a small laugh, "What bullshit, to say I'm not attracted to you."

She blinked at him, so startled she almost toppled over.

He shook his head. "You're not blind and you sure as hell aren't stupid. You *know* I want you."

"You do?"

"I do."

He briefly kissed her, but it was enough to make her breathless. "Even now," she questioned, "with us standing here in my kitchen and everyone else right outside? Even though I haven't just jumped you and dragged you to the ground?"

"Is that what you thought?" A sexy smile played with his mouth, making her heart punch. "That just because you took me by surprise and actually got me flat on my back was the only reason I acted as I did last week?"

Ignoring the part about taking him by surprise, Wynn nodded. The how and why of their interlude last week wasn't important. Not when right now, all she really, *really* wanted was for him to kiss her again. But he just kept staring at her mouth while his big rough thumbs stroked her cheeks and that was so nice, too, she held still and didn't dare complain or ask for more.

"Wynn, you did just take me by surprise, you know that don't you? You're strong, honey, but there's no way in hell you'd best me in a physical confrontation."

"Okay."

He laughed, a low husky sound, and shook his head. "You're placating me." And he kissed her again. "You're something else, you know that? I've never met a woman who wanted a man, yet continued to insult his manhood with every other breath."

"Your, ah, manhood?" Her gaze skipped down his body to his lap. He lifted her chin, keeping her from that erotic perusal while making a "tsking" sound.

"My machismo," he explained, "my masculinity." He tipped her face up and kissed her throat, the soft spot beneath her ear.

Wynn's toes curled inside her gym shoes.

"One of these days," he added while licking her ear and driving her insane, "I'm going to prove it to you."

"Yes." She had no idea what he wanted to prove, but whatever it might be, she was all for it.

His laugh was a little more robust this time. He

looked at her, studied her dazed eyes and nodded. "All right. So, the challenge is made. What am I to do? I'm just a man after all, and I can only take so much without caving in."

He said all that with a wicked smile.

She said, "What?"

"Will you be at your hammock tonight?"

That caught her attention. Hope and excitement flared inside her. "Yes. Sure, of course."

"So anxious." He grinned and kissed her bottom lip. "I know this is wrong, I swear I do. But damn I want you. You're making me nuts, woman."

His machismo sounded just fine to her attuned ears. She smiled dreamily. "You're making me nuts, too. I tried to leave you alone, to let you get used to the idea of me..."

"Ha!" Shaking his head, smiling, Zack said, "That'd take a lifetime."

She liked the sound of that. A lifetime with Zack. With each day, with every damn minute, she was more attracted to him, in a million different ways.

Seeing her expression, his hands gentled and he waggled her head. "Wynn, I'm not making any promises about anything. If we meet tonight, it's strictly for sex."

Her hopes plummeted, but the excitement was still there. She bit her lip, undecided what to do. On the one hand, she'd never been one for casual sex.

But on the other, she'd never wanted a man like she wanted Zack.

And then suddenly there was a shrill yell from the

yard and Zack moved with a blur of speed. He was outside before Wynn could catch her breath. Recognizing Dani's squeaky little voice, now filled with sobs, she quickly followed.

They found Dani held in Josh's arm, screaming her heart out. Josh, a study of frantic concern, blurted, "She got stung by a bee!"

Bo and Marc and Clint stood in a circle around Josh, wringing their hands and fretting like old women. The sight would have been laughable if it hadn't been for the fat tears streaming down Dani's cheeks.

Zack took Dani and cradled her close to his chest. "Shh, honey, it's okay."

Josh lifted her foot and peered at it. "The stinger is out," he said, and his voice shook.

It amused Wynn that five large overgrown men would quake at a child's cry. Good grief, their panic would feed her own and the whole yard would soon be bawling.

"Is she allergic to stings?" Wynn asked, and both Zack and Josh said, "No."

She walked up to Dani and touched her tiny foot. In soft, soothing tones, she said, "If you think you're hurt, just think how the poor bee feels." She began steering Zack toward the patio. He hugged Dani so close she could barely get her head off his shoulder.

"I don't care about the dumb bee," Dani said, and hiccuped over her tears.

"That's good," Wynn told her, "because he's a goner now. Once they sting someone, that's all she wrote."

Dani looked mollified by that notion. "Really?"

"Yep. They can't grow a stinger back, and what good is a bee without a stinger? Zack, sit down here with her and I'll turn on the hose. The cold water will make it feel better." And to Dani, "You feel like soaking those little pink toes?"

Dani smiled and nodded, but her bottom lip still quivered.

Zack sat, rocking his daughter in his arms.

Wynn shook her head and fetched the hose. After about half a minute of freezing cold water running over her tiny foot, Dani struggled to sit up. She took one look at Zack, and patted his chest. "I'm 'kay."

He hugged her close, half-laughing, but still shaken. He also kissed her foot, then had to move so Josh could kiss it, too. Dani accepted the healing kisses as her due.

Zack kissed her one more time, then asked, "Dani, why did you have your shoes off?"

Evidently, this was something forbidden, for Dani summoned a pathetic, apologetic look, and then pointed at Bo. "I was tryin' on his shoes."

Bo took an appalled step back and his entire face darkened with guilt. "My shoes!"

"They're so big," Dani explained, looking down at her lap and giving another little sob. "Even bigger than Daddy's."

Everyone looked at Zack's feet. He muttered, "Size twelve."

Bo, still flushed with guilt, shrugged. "Thirteens," he admitted. "She's right, they are bigger."

Wynn had been stationed by the hose, watching the byplay, the way everyone looked from Zack's feet to Bo's and then to Dani's, doing some sort of bizarre comparison.

Her emotions had been on a roller-coaster ride since meeting Zack, keeping her on edge. Now the idea of a bunch of gargantuan men comparing foot sizes with a child who was so petite she barely reached any of their knees, just struck Wynn funny. She burst out laughing and couldn't stop. When everyone stared toward her, she laughed even harder.

On the edge of embarrassment, no doubt afraid he was the object of hilarity, Bo chuckled, too. Of course, that made Clint and Marc laugh. Dani finally started to giggle, drawn to the sound of the hilarity, though likely her humor wasn't for the same reasons. And with laughter being so contagious, within minutes everyone roared. Dani bounced on Zack's lap, her sting totally forgotten.

Watching Zack laugh was a special delight. Wynn had the feeling he didn't often give in to great displays of any kind of outward emotion. He wasn't, according to Josh, a man who lost his temper or his control.

Yet, with her he'd gone from one extreme to another. Surely, that counted for something. What, she didn't know, but perhaps she'd find out tonight.

Now that she'd made up her mind, she could hardly wait.

8

ZACK CHECKED on Dani one last time. Her tiny foot stuck out from under the sheet, and from the glow of the hall light he could just make out the rainbow print bandage she'd insisted on putting over her bee sting. He bent and kissed her toes, then tucked the foot away.

Dani stirred and stretched. "Daddy?"

A lump in his throat nearly strangled him. She only called him "daddy" when she was very tired, or hurt. He sat on the edge of the bed and smoothed her cheek. "Yeah, sweetie. It's me."

She yawned hugely, then reached for his hand. "We had a swell time today."

Smiling at the way she consistently phrased everything as a statement, Zack said, "Yes, we did."

"I really like Wynn."

"Do you?"

She nodded against her pillow. "You do, too."

Zack hesitated. His daughter had never played matchmaker in her life, so this particular statement totally took him by surprise. He said finally, "I like her fine."

"I like her more than fine. She's the funnest."

"Brat," Zack teased, and asked, "More fun than me?"

"The funnest *woman*," she clarified, and yawned yet again. "I'm gonna keep her."

Her voice had been faint, on the edge of sleep, but still he heard. "Dani? What do you mean you're going to keep her?"

"I want her to be mine," his half-awake daughter announced.

This was something totally new, like the feminine napkin discussion and Zack just knew he was going to start running into more of these torturous episodes. Heart pounding, he asked, "Yours, like as a friend?"

"Uh-huh. And a rela...retal..."

"Relative?"

"Yeah. That."

"She's not our relative, Dani. Remember, I explained relatives to you."

"I know. But she could be a wife and a mommy."

Zack stared at his daughter, and if he hadn't been sitting, he'd have fallen down. Dani's eyes were closed, her cheek nestled into her pillow.

Her sweet little mouth curled into a pleased smile when she said, "And we could have a brother." She peeked one eye open. "I want a brother."

"Honey..."

"A brother like Conan."

God forbid!

"I'd help with diapers and stuff."

"I know you would, sweetheart. But things like brothers take a lot of time."

She closed her eyes again and sighed. "Josh likes Wynn, too."

Zack froze, and found himself asking, "You think so?"

"Maybe he wants a brother." Her brow puckered. "I mean a son."

Zack had tried to talk to Josh about his interest in Wynn, but he hadn't had the chance. By the time Wynn's friends had left, which would have afforded some privacy, Josh had been ready to go, too.

He sat there thinking, recalling what Bo had told him. Wynn didn't date, and she very seldom showed sexual interest in men. Her reaction to Zack, according to those who knew her best, was extreme. Zack had been a little disconcerted to realize they all knew of Wynn's pursuit, but they said it was because she acted so differently with him. In the normal course of things, she pretended to be one of the guys.

Marc had warned him that Wynn was an uncommon woman, who looked at the world in an uncommon way.

As if he'd needed the warning! He'd already figured that out firsthand. Her flirting skills were nonexistent. She said what she wanted, and left Zack to deal with the shock.

Clint had added that she was a good sport, but still hated to lose. At anything. If she wanted Zack, then it'd be difficult to dissuade her.

And they all agreed, she wanted Zack.

He smiled. Wynn's approach was bold, but also refreshing. And now that he believed the reaction was as unique for her as it was for him, his resistance had disappeared.

Zack sat quietly, contemplating all he'd learned today, along with his daughter's sentiments until he heard her breathing even into a light snore. He kissed her forehead and stood. Her bedroom window was open, letting in a cool breeze and plenty of fresh air.

Zack went to the window and looked out. As she'd promised, Wynn sat in the hammock, waiting. At the sight of her, he felt the rush of his blood and the swelling of muscles.

There was a lot to consider, especially his daughter's growing attachment to a woman totally unsuitable for any type of permanency. But for now, none of that seemed to matter.

For now, he had to have her.

He left his daughter's room in a silent rush, closing the door softly behind him. He'd already removed his shoes so his bare feet made no sound as he moved through the house and out the back door. The grass felt soft and cool as he crossed through the darkness to Wynn. As he went, he unbuttoned his shirt, letting the evening breeze drift over his heated flesh.

What he planned, what *they* planned, felt wicked and enticing and so sexual he was already hard.

She stood with her back to him, her arms wrapped tight around her middle when he finally reached her. "Wynn."

Whirling so fast she almost lost her balance, she

gasped, "I didn't hear you!" and in the next breath, with relief, "I was afraid you'd changed your mind."

Her lack of self-protection shook him; she put her heart on the line without reserve, and he felt her trust like a deep responsibility—a responsibility he didn't want. "I had to get Dani settled down."

Her eyes a faint glow in the light of the moon, Wynn looked toward his house. "Will she be all right in there alone?"

"Dani sleeps like a bear hibernating. But if she should wake up, she'll look in the hot tub for me. We'd see the patio light."

With her arms still squeezed around herself, she nodded. "That's good."

"Are you nervous?"

"A little." She shifted her feet, moving a tiny bit closer to him. "I've never had a sexual assignation before."

Zack smiled. "Me, either."

"No?"

"I don't bring women to the house because of Dani. This is her home and I would never do that. My work schedule is crazy enough that when I get time to be with her, I don't generally like to waste it with women."

"Waste it with women," she repeated slowly, as if figuring out the meaning to his words. "You haven't dated much since your wife died?"

"More recently than ever before." He'd been bride hunting, so it had been necessary. "Not that more means very much."

"I know you haven't been celibate."

He laughed at her incredulity. "What is it about you, Wynn, that you can amuse me at the most awkward times?"

She frowned. "I didn't mean to amuse you. And what's awkward about now?"

Zack touched her cheek, let his fingers trail down to her throat and her bare shoulder. She wore a dark sleeveless cotton dress—like a long shirt—and she felt warm and very soft. "This is awkward because I'm so turned-on I can barely breathe."

"Zack." She rushed against him, clinging to him, her hands strong on his shoulders, her body pressed full length against his own. "How...how are we going to manage this? Not only haven't I had any assignations, but I've never made love in a hammock before either." She lifted her head and he felt her gentle breath on his jaw. "Have you?"

"No, but it doesn't matter." He kissed her, a light kiss to her temple, the bridge of her nose, the corner of her mouth. "Are you one hundred percent certain of this, Wynn?"

She offered a slight hesitation that just about made his heart stop, then nodded. "Very certain."

"Thank God." He kissed her, tasting her excitement and her urgency, which almost mirrored his own. Her lips were soft, and they parted for his tongue. Kissing Wynn was...well, it was definitely exciting. But it was more than that. Kissing her affected him everywhere, making his head spin and his abdomen cramp and his thighs ache.

He slid one hand down her back to her lush behind and pulled her in close, then groaned when she rubbed herself against his erection.

They both panted.

Wynn went to work on getting his shirt pushed off his shoulders. He shrugged it off, letting it land in the grass. With a sound of approval her fingers spread wide over his chest, tangling in his body hair, caressing his muscles, teasing over his nipples.

He backed her into the tree and briefly pinned her there with his hips, grinding himself into her. He filled his hands with her breasts and their mouths meshed hotly, licking and sucking. Zack felt her pointed nipples, felt the lurch of her body as he gently rolled one sensitive tip. It wasn't enough. He caught the narrow shoulder straps and pulled them down to her elbows. She slipped her arms free and the dress bunched at her waist.

Moonlight made her breasts opalescent, made her nipples look dark and ripe. Shuddering with lust, he bent his head and drew her right nipple deeply into the heat of his mouth.

"Zack!"

"Shhh...." He licked and tasted and plucked with his lips. The husky sounds she made, hungry and real and encouraging, fired his lust. He lifted her dress.

She wasn't wearing panties.

"*Damn.*" Zack stared at her wide eyes while his

hands moved over the silky skin of her bottom. He closed his eyes, exploring her, relishing the feel of her, the carnality of the moment. "Damn, Wynn," he said again.

Her voice was a breathless, uncertain murmur. "I...I thought underwear might just be in the way, and I didn't know if..."

Zack went to his knees and pushed the dress higher.

Startled, Wynn tried to step away, but the tree was at her back and Zack held her securely. "*What* are you *doing?*" She sounded frantic as she pulled at his shoulders.

"It's dark." Zack glanced up, saw her embarrassment even in the night shadows and asked gently, "No man's ever kissed you here?"

She smacked at his shoulder. "*Zack*," she hissed, and to his amazement, she looked around.

He couldn't help but laugh. "It's a little late to be worrying about voyeurs, Wynn."

"But..." She held his shoulders securely, as if she could keep him away. "You can't do that out here!"

"We can have intercourse, but not oral sex?"

She gasped, thoroughly scandalized by his words, and quickly looked around the deserted yard again. Zack loved it. For once he had the upper hand and no way in hell would he give it up. Especially since he was dying to taste her, to hear her moan out a climax.

He taunted her, saying, "You'll like this Wynn. And so will I."

"I don't know..."

Knotting the dress in a fist, he anchored it high at the small of her back. He cursed the clouds that made the moon insufficient light. He wanted to see all of her, not just hints of her, curves and hollows exaggerated by the shadows. He wanted to see each soft pink inch of her sex, the dent of her navel, the dimples in her knees.

He groaned; what he could see was spectacular. Her thighs were beautiful, sleek and firm and now pressed tightly together as he stroked them each in turn. He looked up at her breasts, as large as the rest of her, full and white.

He couldn't tell the color of the hair on her mound, but he guessed it to be the same as her eyebrows, slightly darker than the honey brown hair on her head. He sifted his fingers through her curls and heard her indistinct whimper of excitement. Leaning close, he pressed his cheek to her belly as he touched her.

Her belly...well he'd always loved female bellies. To Zack, they epitomized femininity, soft and slightly rounded and smooth. Wynn's belly was extremely sexy. He felt her quiver and turned his face, kissing her, licking her navel; all the while his fingers continued to pet her. Nothing more, just petting, but it made him so damn hot he felt burned.

Night sounds closed in around them, the hum of insects, the rustle of a soft breeze through the treetops. Clouds crossed the moon repeatedly, first softening the light, then obliterating it. The air felt thick, charged, damp.

"Zack, I don't know if I like this..."

"You'll like it," he assured her in a rough whisper. He trailed his fingers lower, cupping her, then working his fingertips between her clenched thighs. Her buttocks pressed back against his fist holding her dress. Zack urged her forward again.

He felt her. Her lips were swollen, warm and slick. He touched her gently, sliding back and forth until she grew even wetter, then he pushed one finger deep inside.

Her knees locked and she made a long, raw sound of surprised pleasure. "This," she rasped, "isn't at all what I expected."

Had she expected him to be *sweet*, Zack wondered? Had she thought to be the aggressor? The idea tormented him. Her misconceptions about him could be alternately amusing and enraging.

"Open your legs, Wynn."

Her head tipped back against the tree and she said, "The way you say that..." She looked down at him. "It really turns me on."

Zack stared up at her, his finger still pressed deep into the heat of her body, clenched by her muscles, and she wanted to talk? "Open them, Wynn."

After a long look and a shuddered breath, she obliged him. Zack damn near came watching her long legs shift apart—for him.

"What will you do?" she asked, and she sounded almost as excited as he felt.

"This," he told her, sliding his finger deeper, then slowly pulling it out. Her muscles gripped him, held on tight. He worked a second finger into her. "You're tight, Wynn."

She reached above her head and clasped a branch for support, then moved her legs wider apart. "You expected something else from a big girl like me?"

"I never know what to expect from you." That was certainly the truth. Tired of talking, Zack kissed her thigh, her hipbone. "You smell incredible."

She groaned a protest when he pulled his fingers from her, until he began petting her again, spreading her wetness upward, over her clitoris.

She cried out, and her whole body jerked. He continued to touch her, circling and plucking and stroking. Her hips thrust toward him, her whole body straining. He could smell her, the fresh, pungent scent of aroused woman.

It had been so long, too damned long. He leaned forward, opened her further with his fingers, and drew her into his mouth, savoring her with a raw sound of hunger and satisfaction. The contact was so startling, so intense, she tried to lurch away, but he gripped her hips in his hands and held her pinned to the tree while he got his fill.

She gave up and with his support, her thighs fell open further, giving him better access, which he quickly accepted, licking and sucking at her hot sweet flesh. Her hands tangled hard in his hair, pulling him closer still.

Zack's heart punched hard in his chest and his cock

strained in his jeans. He couldn't wait another second. He stood and turned her. "Hold onto the tree."

Panting, rigid, she looked at him over her shoulder and said, "What..?"

Zack had his jeans opened and the condom out in a heartbeat. He rolled it on, moaning at the sensation of the rubber on his erection, his teeth gritted with the effort of holding back. He stepped up to her, slipped his fingers under her to open her for his entry, and took a soft love bite of her shoulder while he pressed in.

Wynn flattened her hands on the rough bark, bracing herself, groaning with him. He wanted to touch her everywhere, and did. He felt her breasts, rolled her nipples, stroked her belly and below, fingering her until she cried and relaxed and he could sink deep into her.

"Oh yeah," he rumbled, finally where he'd wanted to be almost from the first second he saw her. He had to catch his breath and his control before he could start the rhythm they both needed. "Tilt your hips. Push back against me, Wynn. That's it, sweetheart."

He gripped her hips and helped her. When she caught the frenzied rhythm, he returned to pleasuring her, one hand on her breasts, one between her legs.

Sweat dampened his back though the night was cool. He squeezed his eyes shut and concentrated on not coming, on not giving in to the raging need to let go. He wanted her with him, wanted to know that she'd climaxed, that he'd satisfied her. He pressed his face into her shoulder while his every muscle grew taut and rippled and suddenly she went still, holding her breath.

"Yes, Wynn," he urged her, knowing he was a goner, that he'd last maybe two seconds more and that was it. Her head dropped forward between her stiffened arms and her breath came out in a long, low earthy moan that obliterated any last thread of his control. She didn't scream, but at the end she said his name on a seductive, satisfied whisper of sound that licked along his spine.

He shuddered as he came, holding her tight and pounding into her, not the least bit worried about hurting her, not when she continued to roll her hips sinuously against him, continued to make soft sounds of completion and satisfaction.

A big woman was nice, better than nice.

He slumped into her, which made her slump into the tree. They both struggled for breath.

A few seconds later, she groaned and shifted the tiniest bit. "Zack?"

"Hmmm." Their skin felt melded together, her back to his chest, her sweet backside to his groin, the front of his hairy thighs to the smooth backs of hers. He didn't want to move, not ever.

"The tree isn't all that comfortable," she complained. "Do you think we can totter over there to the hammock?"

His legs were still jerking in small spasms. His heart hadn't completely slowed its mad gallop yet. There was a low ringing still in his ears.

He felt stripped bare down to his soul. His lungs burned. "Yeah, sure. No problem."

Determined not to crumble, he straightened slowly.

He felt like an old man with arthritis, very unsure of his ability to stay on his feet. He removed the condom, dropped it into the grass with the mental reminder to dispose of it later, then tugged his jeans back up.

All that took more effort than he could spare and he nearly collapsed again. Wynn didn't help, not when she turned and leaned into him. She was a woman, but she was no lightweight. He remembered lifting his petite wife after sex and holding her in his arms. Ha!

Zack eyed the hammock that wasn't too far away considering they were against the tree supporting it at one end. He slung an arm around Wynn and fell into the canvas. She laughed as the hammock swung wildly, almost tossing them both, but when they stayed more in it than on the ground she snuggled around until she was mostly on top of him.

"Will the ropes hold both of us, do you think?"

"If not, I'll buy you a new one."

"You will not." She leaned up and looked at his mouth, then touched him with a gentle fingertip. In the most sweetly feminine voice he'd ever heard from her, Wynn said, "I really liked what you did."

Zack closed his eyes and grinned. She'd damn near yanked him bald with her enthusiasm, so he'd assumed as much.

He said, "I told you so."

"It seemed sort of...kinky."

Still grinning, he said, "It only seems kinky the first time. Trust me."

"Did you like it?"

He opened one eye. She looked uncertain. "My only complaint is that once again you pushed me over the edge."

"I didn't!"

"I wanted to spend more time tasting you. More time hearing you make all those sweet little squeaking womanly noises."

He was dead to the world, barely able to drum up a little teasing, and she had the energy to slug him in the shoulder. Luckily he was still numb so it didn't hurt.

"I do *not* squeak!"

He smoothed his hand down her back, discovered her dress was still hiked up, and patted her bare bottom. It was a nice big bottom, filling his large hand. "You squeak and you moan and I like it."

"You did your own share of moaning."

"Men don't moan," he informed her, "they groan. There's a definite difference."

"Whatever you say."

He smiled. "I like how you taste, too."

She ducked her head and rubbed herself against him.

Because he was too comfortable, too replete, he admitted, "At least I should finally sleep tonight."

"Are you saying you haven't slept well lately?"

He used both hands to hold on to her backside and anchor her close. "No. I've been as restless as a horny teenager."

That had her laughing, but she quickly sobered. "My parents are moving in tomorrow."

Zack yawned. "Yeah, I remember."

Turning shy on him, she curled her finger in and around his chest hair and said, "I was hoping we could maybe do this again."

Her meaning sank in and Zack stilled. Ah hell, he couldn't possibly be expected to get his fill of her in one lousy night! He'd been too primed and ended it too quickly. He hadn't luxuriated in her, hadn't explored her as he'd meant to, as he'd thought about doing.

A week, maybe two weeks, would take the edge off. But not one damn night.

"May I assume by your frown that you want to do this again?" Wynn asked.

Zack lifted his head enough to feast on her mouth in a long, slow, wet, eating kiss. When he released her, they were both panting again. "Yeah," he said, "you can assume that."

Wynn tucked her head into his shoulder. She had one leg bent across his abdomen, the other stretched out to the bottom of the hammock. Zack had one leg on the outside of hers, the other over the side with his foot firmly planted on the ground so he could keep them swaying.

He mulled over a few possibilities and then asked, "Are your parents the protective sort?"

She snorted. "No."

He didn't like how quickly she answered that. Parents should be protective, especially of a daughter living alone. But since he had his own plans, he didn't say so. "I've got stuff planned tomorrow and Tuesday. But Wednesday I should get home from work around eight.

By nine-thirty I can have Dani tucked away." His mind conjured all sorts of erotic possibilities and he growled, "Is it possible you could come visit me, say to use the hot tub, and they wouldn't check up on you?"

Though Wynn didn't move, the rushing of her heartbeat gave away her excitement. "They wouldn't think a thing of it. They're used to me being pals with guys."

That made Zack chuckle. Damn, she tickled him with her strange replies and stranger relationships. "It'll be dark by then. I'll watch for you."

"Let's make it ten o'clock. My parents will be in bed by then."

Her position left her soft sex open and vulnerable to him. Zack trailed his fingertips over her bottom cheeks until he could feel the heat of her. He pressed. "Have you ever made love in a hot tub?"

"No." She reared up to glower at him, and the heat in her eyes was a combination of suspicion and arousal. Because of where and how he touched her, her voice shook when she demanded, "Have you?"

Zack thought she might be jealous, and oddly enough, he liked that. "No." He could see her face clearly now, the incredible hazel eyes, the long lashes and the very kissable mouth. "I've never made love against a tree before either. Or in a hammock."

He touched her tender lips, still swollen and wet from their lovemaking, then pushed his middle finger into her.

She panted. "Me, neither."

With her practically straddling his abdomen, Zack

kicked the hammock again, making it rock. She grabbed his shoulders for support. He looked at her naked breasts bobbing and swaying before him and immediately grew hard. "I just might prove successful at all three."

Wynn made a low sound of agreement. "Based on what I've seen so far, I wouldn't be at all surprised."

"I have another condom in my pocket."

"A man who comes prepared. Incredible."

Zack started to laugh at that, but then she came down over him, her breasts pressing into his chest, and she kissed him and all he could think about was making love to her again. Wednesday seemed a long way off, so he'd have to make this last. And to do that, he'd have to slow her down.

"Wynn?"

"Hmm?" She continued to kiss his mouth, his chin, his jaw.

"Scoot up."

She stilled, lifted her head to stare at him. "Why?"

"Because I want to kiss your breasts. And then your belly—you have an adorable belly by the way. And then maybe I'll even nibble on this sweet rear end of yours."

Her eyes almost crossed; she swallowed hard. "Are you going to...do what you did to me again?"

He nodded slowly. "Oh yeah. You can bet I am."

Wynn froze, caught her breath, and with barely contained excitement, she attacked him. For Zack, it was the strangest sensation to laugh and lust at the same time. Strange, but also addictive.

It was well past midnight before he finally dragged his spent, satisfied body into his own house. And as he suspected, he no sooner collapsed onto the bed than he was sound asleep, with a very stupid smile on his face.

9

"DARLING!"

Wynn jerked so hard at the sound of that loud, wailing voice, she lost her footing on the ladder. It shifted against the gutter, making her yelp and attempt to grab for the roof, but it was too late. Her hands snatched at nothingness.

As if in slow motion, the ladder pulled farther away from the house and Wynn found herself pedaling the air for several suspended seconds before she landed in the rough evergreen bushes with a hard thud. The wooden ladder crashed down on top of her.

"Ohmigod! Wynn! Wynn!"

A flash of red satin blurred in front of her eyes as her father knelt in front of her. The sunlight caught his diamond earring and nearly blinded her. "My baby! Are you okay?"

Her head was ringing and her side hurt like hell. She had a mouthful of leaves and something sharp poked at her hip. Her father began picking debris from her hair, tsking and fussing until her mother showed up and shoved him aside.

"Dear God, you nearly killed her, Artemus!"

Wearing faded cutoffs and a colorful tie-dye smock,

Wynn's mother leaned over her. "It's a good thing we're here, Wynonna. You look hurt."

Wynn could only stare. A good thing? She wouldn't be hurt if her father hadn't startled her so. She hadn't even heard their car arrive. Of course, her thoughts had been on Zack, on that mind-blowing episode the night before, not on her parents' extended visit. She'd slept little last night, too busy going over and over all the wonderful things Zack had done to her and with her.

Her mother sat back on her heels. "Artemus, will you look at her? I think she hit her head."

Artemus leaned down and waved his hand in front of her face. "Yoo-hoo, princess? Baby, can you hear us?"

Suddenly Artemus was shoved aside again, but not by her mother. Zack, wearing only jeans that weren't properly fastened and a very rugged shadowing of beard stubble, crouched down in front of her. "Wynn?" Unlike her parents, his voice was gentle and concerned. He touched her cheek, which she realized had been scraped raw by a bush. "No, don't move, sweetheart. Just hold still and let me make certain you're okay."

Sweetheart? She glanced at her parents and saw them both staring with speculation. Oh dear. Wynn blinked at Zack. "Um...what are you doing here?" It was very early still, not quite seven, and Zack should have been home getting ready for work.

"I was making my coffee when I saw you climb the damn ladder. Before I could get dressed and tell you how stupid you were being, you fell."

Her mother asked, "You were making coffee naked?"

Without looking at her, Zack said, "No, in my underwear."

A wave of heat washed over Wynn. Her parents began staring even harder.

Wynn cleared her throat. "My father startled me."

"Well!" Artemus took immediate exception to that accusation. "If your hair wasn't in your eyes, maybe you would have seen me coming and you wouldn't have *been* startled!"

Zack turned to him to say something, and went mute. Her father was in top form today. He wore a red silk shirt, open at the collar to show a profuse amount of curly chest hair. He had two rings on his fingers, a gold chain around his neck and the big diamond earring he almost never removed. His pressed dark-blue designer jeans were so tight they fit like his skin, and his low boots were polished to a shine. His golden brown hair, so unlike Wynn's, was parted in the middle and hung nearly to his shoulders.

At Zack's scrutiny, he tossed his head and huffed.

Zack snapped his mouth shut and turned back to Wynn without uttering a word. "Where are you hurt?"

"Nowhere. I'm okay." But when she started to sit up, she winced and Zack caught her shoulders.

"No, let me check you."

"Daddy?"

Dani stood there, still in her nightgown and holding a fuzzy yellow blanket. Wynn smiled at her. "I'm okay munchkin."

"You're in the bushes."

"Luckily they broke my fall."

Dani smiled. "I saw you on the roof. I wanna get on the roof, too."

Zack turned so quickly everyone jumped. "Dani, if I catch you even thinking such a thing you'll be grounded in your room for a month!"

"Wynn did it."

Zack ground his teeth together. When he turned to Wynn, his expression was no longer so concerned. Now he looked furious. "Wynn will tell you what a dumb stunt that was, won't you, Wynn?"

Everyone stared at her. Her parents looked particularly interested in seeing her response, and she knew it was because they expected her to chew Zack up and spit him out in little bits. Never, ever, did she let anyone speak to her as he did.

But there was Dani, watching and waiting, and the thought of the child trying to get on a roof made her skin crawl. "I should have waited until there was someone to hold the ladder steady for me, Dani. Sometimes I do things without really thinking about them. It's a bad habit."

Her mother gasped and her father pretended to stagger. After a long second, Zack gave her a thankful nod.

Relieved, Wynn said, "Mom, Dad, this is my neighbor Zack Grange and his daughter Dani. Zack is a paramedic."

"Well, that explains everything," her father said with facetious humor.

Wynn winced again as Zack pressed his fingertips

over her side. She said quickly, "Zack, my mother Chastity and my father Artemus."

Dani said, "I like Wynn lots."

"We're rather fond of her, too," Artemus said, and he patted Dani's head, then frowned at her hair.

Zack paid no attention to the introductions. "Let me get your shirt up and see what you've done."

Chastity laughed.

"No, Zack, really I'm fine, I just... Zack stop it..."

Chastity said, "Oh be still, Wynonna. Let the man have a look."

Zack looked.

A long bloody scratch ran up and over her ribs almost to her breast. Zack looked furious. "This needs to be cleaned."

"I'll take care of it as soon as you *let-me-out-of-the-bushes!*"

He began checking her arms, her legs. Wynn, peeved at being the center of attention, scrambled out of his reach, gaining more scratches in the bargain. Using the side of the house for support, she stood.

Her efforts ended in a gasp and she almost dropped again. Zack caught her under the arms. "What is it? Your leg?"

"No." She squeezed her eyes shut and whimpered. Damn damn damn. There was no help for it. Drooping, she said, "It's my toe."

"Your toe?" her father repeated.

"My baby toe." She was balanced on her left leg, so Zack rightfully assumed she'd injured her right toe.

"I'm going to lift you," he told her. "Tell me if I hurt you."

"Zack!" The whole situation was going from bad to worse. "You can't lift me."

"She weighs more than I do," her father said.

Wynn gasped. "I do not!" She tried to slap him, but he ducked aside.

In the next instant she found herself securely held against Zack's bare chest. His arms didn't shake and his legs were steady. He didn't appear the least bit strained.

Awareness mushroomed inside her.

She couldn't remember the last time anyone had lifted her up. Even Conan didn't do it anymore, claiming she was too big, and he could easily bench-press four-fifty.

It felt kinda nice. Dumb but nice.

She wrapped her arms around his neck, but said, "You can put me down, Zack."

He stepped out of the bushes. "Dani, come with me into Wynn's house. We'll get you dressed in just a minute."

"We'll be late," Dani predicted with an adult sigh, and skipped after him.

Wynn looked over Zack's shoulder and saw her parents watching the display with fascination. She groaned. "This is awful."

"Wynn?"

"What?"

"You'll notice I'm not even breathing hard."

She looked at him, his hair mussed and his eyes still heavy from sleep. His sleek, hard shoulders were warm and his chest was solid. He smelled delicious. "I did notice that."

"And I'm not straining, either."

Despite her humiliation at having fallen off a ladder, shocking her parents and making Zack run late, she smiled. "Superhero."

He grinned. "C'mon Dani. You can open the door for me. I think Wynn's parents are a little confused by all this."

"They're confused," Wynn responded, "by the sight of a male neighbor feeling me up in the bushes and toting me around with a lot more familiarity than has ever been exhibited in the past."

"I wasn't *feeling you up*. I was checking you over. There's an enormous difference."

"Yeah, well, I could tell by my parents' expressions, they considered it one and the same."

Zack paused to look down at her. His breath smelled of toothpaste and was warm. "I was watching you through that window, cursing you if you want the truth, and when I saw you fall, my heart almost stopped."

At the husky tone of his voice, something inside Wynn turned to mush—probably her brains. But it sounded as if he cared about her, at least enough to not want her to break her neck.

Wynn drew a breath. "I'm sorry," she answered, her voice just as husky. "I didn't hear them drive up."

"Mmmm." Zack stared at her mouth. "Had your mind on other things did you?"

"She was daydreamin'," Dani said and pulled the door open with exaggerated impatience.

"Is that right?" Zack stepped into the kitchen and went through to the family room. "Were you daydreaming, Wynn? About what, I wonder."

She muttered close to his ear, "As if you didn't know," and saw his small satisfied smile.

He lowered her carefully to the couch. "Let me get your shoe and sock off."

"I can do it."

Of course he ignored her wishes and untied her laces. "Zack, my feet are probably sweaty by now. I've been up and working since about five."

"Do you ever not work?" Pushing aside her fretful hands, he eased her sneaker off. "Sweaty," he confirmed as he peeled her sock away and began examining her toe.

Wynn stretched up to see. Dani stood beside her and patted her shoulder.

Her poor little baby toe was already black and blue and the bruising had climbed halfway up her foot. It was swollen and looked awful. Seeing it made it hurt worse, but she forced a laugh and said, "Big and sweaty. Betcha wish now you'd left my sock on."

"Damn, Wynn," Zack muttered, touching her foot with a heart wrenching gentleness. "It's definitely broken. You need to ice it, then get it taped. Can your doctor see you today?"

"For a baby toe?" She snorted. "Don't be ridiculous." Wynn seriously doubted she could hobble her way to the doctor right now, the way her foot felt. How one small toe could cause so much pain was a mystery.

The kitchen door opened and closed and her parents joined them at the couch. Her father went straight for her head and began trying to groom her hair. Her mother asked, "Do you have any herbal tea? That always helps."

Zack looked pained, then resigned. "I need to be getting to work. But she has a broken toe, maybe even a broken foot, so it should be X-rayed. She's also got a lot of cuts and scratches that'll need to be cleaned."

Her father said, "Wynn, Wynn, Wynn."

She swatted his hands away from her hair. "I'm fine, Dad."

Chastity looked Zack over from head to toe and back again. "Well." She smiled. "You run along young man. We're here now and we'll take good care of her."

"You're a hippie," Dani said with awe.

Zack said, "Dani!"

But Chastity laughed. "Did my daughter tell you that?"

Dani nodded. "And you gots rings on your toes."

"Just two rings, but they're made of a special metal that has healing powers. Perhaps I'll put one on Wynn and it'll make her toe heal quicker."

"No!" Zack caught himself and stood. He looked frazzled and harassed and undecided. "No rings."

Then, stressing the point by speaking slowly, he said, "She needs an X-ray."

"Zack," Wynn said, "I'm a big girl."

"Indeed." Her father moved from her hair to Dani's and Dani appeared to love the attention. She even gave Artemus a huge grin.

"I can take care of myself. I'm not an idiot!"

"No, just an intelligent woman who climbs a rickety ladder to the roof before the sun is even all the way up."

"If Dad hadn't snuck up on me..."

"Now don't go blaming me again, darling! Your young man is right. You had no business being on that ladder in the first place." He said all that without looking up, too busy working on Dani's hair.

Zack opened his mouth, then closed it. He shook his head. "Wynn, promise me you'll go get an X-ray."

"But..."

"It's likely just a broken toe and they'll tape it, but it's better to be safe than sorry. Being a physical therapist, you should know this."

She did know it. "Oh, all right."

As if making a decision, Zack said, "I'll check on you tonight. In the meantime, Mrs. Lane, why don't you get her some ice to soak her foot for the swelling? And Mr. Lane, you could maybe get her a phone so she can make the call to the doctor?"

Her parents looked pleased with the direction. Artemus quickly finished fooling with Dani's hair and rushed off. Chastity followed him.

The second they were out of the room, Zack bent over

Wynn. "I wish I had more time, but if I don't get going now, I'll be late."

"I understand. Really, I'm fine."

"When I get home I expect to find you taking it easy."

"Me and my large feet will make a leisurely day of it."

He touched her cheek. "Large feet for a large, beautiful woman."

Now her brain and her bones were mush. She managed a lopsided silly smile.

Zack straightened. "I'll see you tonight."

"I thought you had plans."

"I do." He didn't explain beyond that.

Wynn wanted to ask him what his plans were, but she was afraid he'd be out with another woman. And because she had no exclusive rights to him, she couldn't complain, so she was better off not knowing.

Dani kissed her cheek. "I'll see ya tonight, too. I'll even draw you a picture."

It was then that Wynn noticed Dani's fine, fair hair had been plaited into an intricate braid and tied with a tiny yellow ribbon. She shook her head in wonder. Did her father carry ribbons in his pockets?

She wouldn't be at all surprised.

Zack noticed his daughter's hair, too. He did a quick double take, then said, "Well I'll be."

Dani smiled and kept reaching back to feel it. She looked very pleased with the results. "It's pretty."

Wynn said, "Very pretty!" and meant it.

Chastity hustled back in with a big bowl filled with

ice and several dishcloths over her arm. She dropped onto the foot of the couch, making Wynn groan. To Dani, she asked, "You're the artist who created that masterpiece on the refrigerator?"

Wynn managed a smile to help cover the discomfort of her mother's rough movements. "That's right. Isn't she talented?"

"Very much so." As Chastity wrapped ice in a towel, she said, "You'd love finger paints. Have you ever tried them?"

Both Wynn and Zack winced. "Mom, they're awfully messy."

"So?" She flapped a dismissive hand at Wynn. "You and your cleanliness quirks. She's a child! You can't stifle her creative spirit just because she might get a little paint under her nails." Chastity was gentle as she applied the ice to Wynn's foot.

Watching Zack, Wynn thought he might have jumped her mother if she hadn't shown what he considered adequate care. "I brought my paints with me, Dani. It'll be lovely, you'll see."

Beaming, Dani said, "Thank you!"

Artemus waltzed in with the phone. "Found it!" He handed it to Wynn, along with her small phone book, then turned to Dani. He patted her hair with pride. "Lovely." Then to his daughter, "Wynn," he said, "wouldn't you like for me to do something with your hair while you make your call?"

Wynn said, "No," and her father's face fell with comical precision.

Zack scooped Dani and her blanket into his arms. "We have to run. Wynn, remember what I said."

"Me and my big feet will follow doctor's orders."

There was a general round of farewells, and five seconds later, Zack was gone. Wynn fell back against the couch. Her foot throbbed and ached, her ribs pulled, she itched from all the shrub scratches and now her parents were standing there staring at her with tell-all expectation.

The day had started out being so promising, but now...

She doubted it had dawned on Zack yet, but after all they'd just witnessed, no way would her parents believe a simple visit to the hot tub. Nope, they were eccentric, but they were not dumb.

And they knew sexual chemistry when they witnessed it.

Her mother, pretending a great interest in Wynn's bruised and swollen toes, said, "My, my, my. What a hottie." She slanted Wynn a look and an I'm-onto-you grin.

"Quite virile," her father agreed, while tugging distractedly on his earring and eyeing his wife's legs. Despite years of marriage and the fact that he was more colorful, Artemus remained highly attracted to her mother. He made no effort to hide his sexual willingness, which pretty much started from the time Chastity woke in the morning and ran until she fell asleep at night. It was almost comical.

He visibly pulled himself back to the subject at hand. "I, ah, take it he's single?"

Wynn sank further into the cushions. "Yes."

Silence reigned for only a few seconds, and then her father clasped his hands together and sighed. "Well, the little girl has *fabulous* hair! Or at least she will when I finish with it. All in all, I say they'll be a wonderful addition to the family. What do you think, dear?"

Chastity smiled. "I think we got here just in time to watch the fireworks."

ZACK HEARD the noise from Wynn's house the second he stepped out of his car. Blaring music competed with laughter and the din of loud conversation.

It was six-thirty and he was tired, hungry, worried and rushed. It seemed he'd been running late from the moment he woke that morning, and there'd been no letup since.

He'd started the day by oversleeping. After the excesses of lovemaking the night before, he'd slept like the dead and hadn't even heard his alarm until it had been ringing for almost half an hour. When he got over that disquieting phenomenon, he'd washed his face and brushed his teeth in two minutes flat, then gone for coffee before attempting to put a razor to his throat.

He never had gotten around to shaving, he realized, and now he felt scruffy and unkempt. He rubbed his rough jaw, remembering the trials of the day.

It was as he'd measured coffee that he glanced out the kitchen window and spied Wynn precariously balanced on an old wooden ladder, attempting to clean her gutters. His hair had been on end, his eyes still gritty, his feet bare on the cold linoleum floor, and he lost his temper.

He ran upstairs to awaken Dani, hastily pulled on pants, then ran back downstairs and outside to confront Wynn before she fell and killed herself.

He'd been too late.

It still made him tremble when he remembered opening the door just in time to see her wildly flailing the air as she plummeted to the ground. His stomach cramped anew.

Damned irritating, irrational, provoking female! She was lucky she'd only broken a toe!

He thought about her parents and cringed. "Flaming heterosexual," she'd called her father, and now he knew the description was apt. He'd never met a more flamboyant, dramatic man; his every word and gesture had been exaggerated.

But he'd done a wonderful job with Dani's hair. She'd looked so cute...

Zack shook his head.

Wynn's mother was, as she'd claimed, a hippie. Her long blond hair had streaks of gray, but her figure was still youthful. Wynn had likely gotten her beautiful legs from her mother. Chastity's legs weren't nearly as long, and the rings on her toes were a distraction, but all in all, she was an attractive woman. Loony, but attractive.

After Zack secured Wynn's promise to see a doctor, he'd rushed back home to prepare for work. He left the house right on time. Unfortunately, when he reached Eloise's house to drop off Dani, he'd found the elderly woman ill.

With Dani hovering nearby, Zack did a medical check on Eloise. She was feverish and pale, her pulse too weak. Eloise claimed it was no more than the flu and she warned Dani to beware of her germs. She said she'd been sick off and on all night, so she'd called Zack that morning. But it must have been while he was at Wynn's house, and he hadn't thought to check his answering machine in his hurry to get out the door.

He called his supervisor and explained why he'd be late so one of the men from the shift before could stay over, then he'd bundled Eloise up for a trip to the emergency room. He wasn't willing to take any chances with a woman her age, especially when she looked so weak. While he gathered a few things for her, he'd called Josh, who was off that day.

A woman had answered.

Zack thought about hanging up and calling Del or Mick instead, but Josh retrieved the phone, discovered the dilemma and made plans to pick up Dani at the hospital.

En route to the hospital, Zack got hold of Eloise's granddaughter, who also agreed to meet them there in case Eloise needed to be admitted.

By the time he finally got to work, he was almost two hours late. The women he worked with teased him about his unshaven appearance and harried demeanor.

And throughout it all, he'd thought of Wynn.

She plagued him, making his brain ache and his body hot. He alternately worried about her and her broken toe, and contemplated making love to her again.

He glanced to the front of her house now where the driveway, just visible from his side yard, could be seen overflowing with a variety of vehicles.

A party.

She'd promised him she'd take it easy, that she'd prop her large feet up and rest. Instead, she was having a party.

Zack locked his jaw tight and stomped up to his kitchen stoop. Fine. Whatever. He'd simply ignore her and her irresponsible ways. It wasn't as if he wanted to worry about her, or even think about her.

No, he just wanted to take her again and again, in about a hundred different ways. He wanted to kiss her body all over, starting on her toes and working his way up those sexy shapely legs until he reached her...

"Oh hell." Zack jerked his door open, called out, "I'm home," and was greeted by silence. He suddenly realized there had been no extra cars in *his* driveway, which meant Josh wasn't here with Dani as he said he'd be.

But just to make certain, Zack went through the house. It was empty.

He was so tired he ached, and now he stopped in the middle of the living room and looked around, trying to decide what to do next. Where would Josh be?

He'd left the kitchen door open and now he heard a robust laugh carry across the yards. His mind cramped as he considered the possibilities. With deliberate intent, feeling ill-tempered and irked, he went to the kitchen to look out the window.

There in Wynn's yard were close to a dozen people, including Josh and Dani. A boom box blared from the patio and a badminton net had been set up. A woman he didn't recognize partnered Conan against Marc and Clint, while Bo leaned against a tree and shouted encouragement. It appeared to be a highly competitive game, given the viciousness of the play.

On the patio, he could see Chastity singing as she wielded a long-handled fork on the grill. Artemus, now dressed all in black except for a large silver buckle on his belt that glinted in the late day sun, danced with Dani. His daughter appeared to be wearing one of Chastity's tie-dyed shirts. It hung down to her feet.

Zack looked around without conscious thought and finally located Wynn. She sat on the settee with Josh, her foot in his lap.

Zack felt as though the top of his head had just blown off.

Before he'd even made the decision to move, he was halfway across the lawn, his gaze set on Wynn who was, as yet, unaware of his approach.

Today she was dressed in a pale-peach camisole that almost exactly matched her naked hide, and a pair of loose white drawstring shorts that showed every sexy inch of her long legs and put on display a tiny strip of her delectable belly.

Zack's lungs constricted. When he reached her, he'd—

Conan stepped in front of him. "Whoa, where ya going there, Zack?"

Zack heard a few snickers from behind Conan and knew he'd gained the players' attention.

Conan leaned closer. "The thing is," he whispered, "you look mad as hell and my sister's already been upset all day."

"Yeah," Zack said, still watching Wynn while she smiled and laughed with Josh. "She looks real upset."

Conan blinked, then laughed. "Jealousy is a bitch, ain't it?"

Zack snapped a look at Conan and the man backed up two steps. "Okay, okay," he said, swallowing down a laugh and holding up his hands as if to ward Zack off, "I take it back. You're not jealous."

Zack narrowed his eyes. "What reason would I have to be jealous?"

"None! No reason at all. I mean, believe it or not, Wynn's in pain and... Hey, wait a minute!"

Zack allowed Conan to pull him back around. Wynn was in pain? He couldn't stand it.

Conan laughed. "I'm sorry. Really, I am." Zack vaguely heard the other men laughing and offering comments, but he paid them no mind.

Over his shoulder, Conan shouted, "Shut up, Bo!" To Zack he said, "Ignore Bo. He's been giving Wynn hell all day for being *smitten*. I was about ready to flatten him myself when he finally realized she wasn't taking it well."

Zack drew a deep breath and attempted to ease his

temper. Most times, he didn't have a temper, and he blamed the emergence of one solely on Wynn Lane. She brought out the worst in him.

She also turned him on more than any woman he'd ever known. "Why not?" he asked, hoping he sounded merely calm, not concerned. "What's going on?"

"Whew, finally you sound like a reasonable man." Conan clapped him on the shoulder hard enough to make Zack lose his balance. "At first you were looking like a charging bull. Nostrils flared, eyes red, steam coming out your ears. Bo told me, but I didn't really believe him. I mean, when I met you, you seemed so..."

"Conan."

"Sorry. The folks threw this surprise housewarming party for Wynn, but she's obviously not really up to it. I mean, her damn toe is broken in two places. Two! Can you believe that? Her feet are bigger than most, that's true, but it's still just a baby toe."

Zack closed his eyes and counted to ten, but he still heard the smile in Conan's voice when he continued.

"Your buddy has been fending everyone off, including my parents. He pulled Wynn's foot into his lap after the third person accidentally bumped her and made her yelp. Not a pretty thing to see Wynn yelping."

"Damn."

Conan rubbed his neck, looked up at the fading sun, then back at his teammates who were now clustered together and waiting. He faced Zack again. "The folks mean well. It's just that Wynn never complains much, and she never admits to being hurt, so they don't realize..."

"Dad!" His daughter ran hell-bent toward him, cutting off Conan's explanations. Not that he'd needed to continue; Zack already understood the situation and more than anything he wanted to shake Wynn for putting up such a ridiculous macho show. That was something a man would do, but it wasn't expected of a woman. And despite being hardy and strong, she *was* still a woman.

And damn it, he wanted to protect her.

Dani threw herself at Zack, and he noticed his daughter now wore sandals rather than sneakers. And she had a silver ring on her big toe.

He scooped her up and hugged her to him. "Look at you, Dani," he teased. "Wearing a dress."

She laughed, cupped his face and gave him a loud smooch. "It's not a dress. It's Chastity's. She let me wear it while I finger painted. Ain't it pretty?"

Zack didn't bother correcting her speech, not this time, not while she was so excited and happy. "Yes it is, especially on you."

"Conan said I was a flower child."

"But prettier," Conan clarified.

Zack hugged her again and started toward Wynn. He stopped, turned back to Conan and said, "Thanks."

Conan pretended great relief. "Yeah, anytime. I mean, she's a pain in the ass, but I still love my sister." His voice lowered to something of a warning. "And I wouldn't want anyone to upset her. Or hurt her." He stared at Zack, making sure Zack caught his meaning.

Zack nodded, which was the best reply he could offer, for the time being.

"So," Zack said to his daughter, staring at that silver ring on her toe, "you've had fun today?"

"I've had the bestest time! Artemus is teaching me how to dance and look what he did to my hair!" She primped, turning her head one way and then the other.

Her hair had been braided and then twisted into a coronet with tiny multi-colored crystal beads shaped like flowers pinned into place. Two curling ringlets hung in front of her ears.

Zack felt a lump the size of a grapefruit lodge in his throat at the sight of his daughter's proud smile. Artemus met him at the edge of the patio.

"I need your permission to give her a trim," he said before Zack could greet him. "She has *fabulous* hair, just fabulous. But God only knows how long it's been since it was shaped. It *begs* to be shaped."

Zack looked at Dani, who watched him hopefully. "Do you want your hair shaped?" *Whatever the hell that means.*

She nodded.

"You have my permission."

Artemus clapped his hands in bliss.

Chastity turned to Zack. "Hamburger or hot dog, Zack?"

He eyed this remarkable woman who had managed to birth Wynn. "Do hippies eat meat?"

"Honey, when they're my age, they do any damn thing they want to."

Artemus leaned close to nip her ear. "And there's a lot they want to do, too." He winked at Zack. "Hippies are a delightfully creative lot."

"Ah." Zack grinned, amused by the obvious affection between them. "In that case, I'll take a hamburger. Thank you, ma'am."

"Be ready in a moment."

Josh eased Wynn's foot out of his lap and stood to greet Zack. "How's Eloise?"

"I called the hospital before I left work today. She has bronchitis. With the medicine they gave her, she's feeling a lot more comfortable."

"Has she got anyone to take care of her?"

Zack nodded, not quite looking at Wynn yet. If he looked at her, he'd want to pick her up and pet her and coddle her. *Insane.* As she'd said, it was only a broken toe. "She's going to stay with her granddaughter for a week until she's had time to recuperate."

Dani and Artemus danced past them, moving to the tune of the Beach Boys. "A week, huh? What about the rat? Who's going to watch her?"

Zack glanced at his daughter as she threw back her head and laughed. "I finagled an early vacation week. It wasn't easy, but I got Richards to trade with me."

Josh looked pleased. "So you'll be around the house—" he glanced at Wynn "—day and night, for a week, huh?"

"That's what I just said." Done with that conversational gambit, he knelt down in front of Wynn. "How're you feeling?"

"Fine."

Zack could tell she lied. Her face looked pinched, her mouth tight. He gave her a frown that let her know he knew, and then took Josh's seat. He lifted her foot into his lap to examine her toe.

She wore no shoes and where the bandage didn't cover, he could see the dark, colorful bruises. Her foot still looked swollen and for some dumb reason, he wanted to kiss it. It's what he would have done for Dani, and now he wanted to do it for Wynn, too.

He manfully resisted the urge and met her gaze. "Have you taken anything for pain?"

"Aspirin."

Josh leaned on the armrest next to Wynn and peered down at them both. In a carrying voice, he said, "I'm sure you both know that ice for swelling is good, but soaking it in hot water is best for relieving the pain."

Zack rolled his eyes; Josh knew nil about subtlety, or medical matters.

Wynn just stared at him.

"I was thinking of your hot tub, Zack." Josh cleared his throat and forged on. "A good neighbor would offer to let her use it."

Without turning their way, Chastity said, "Oh, I'm sure he'd have thought of it sooner or later."

Artemus chortled at his wife's wry humor, and then swung Dani in a wide circle, ending their dance with a flourish.

Dani came over and, natural as you please, climbed into Wynn's lap.

Wynn positioned her comfortably, as if she'd been holding Dani since the day she was born.

Zack almost choked on another lump of emotion. Damn it, men didn't get lumps of emotion, and certainly not over something so simple as seeing a neighbor hold his daughter. But Dani was smiling and looking secure and confident in her welcome.

He silently cursed again.

Wynn was *not* the right woman for him. Whenever he'd envisioned the right woman, he'd pictured a woman who was discreet and circumspect and responsible. A woman who'd be a good influence on his daughter and the perfect domestic partner for raising a child.

Wynn was rash and outspoken and irresponsible. She didn't protect herself or think things out before doing them. She knew too many men who knew her too well... No, that wasn't exactly right and he felt guilty for even thinking it. But he found he was the jealous sort when he'd never been before. And that irked him too.

Wynn dressed provocatively, didn't eat right, and her family was beyond strange.

She was big and beautiful and so sexy he couldn't stop thinking about her.

What the hell was he supposed to do?

"Eat," Chastity said as if she'd read his mind. She shoved a paper plate with a loaded hamburger, chips and pickles into his hand. She handed the same to Wynn, and gave Dani a hot dog.

Everyone came in from the badminton game and Conan introduced Zack to his girlfriend, Rachael. She was a pretty, slender woman of medium height. *She* was dressed reasonably in long tan walking shorts and a loose blue polo shirt. And none of the men swatted *her* behind.

However, the second Wynn said she needed to go inside a minute, the guys lined up to carry her. They jokingly compared muscles, trying to decide who was strong enough to bear her weight.

Not giving them a chance to get so much as a pinkie finger on her, Zack lifted Wynn into his lap and then stood. There was a general round of oohing and aahing and muttered respect for his strength.

"What do you bench?" Conan asked, and Zack rolled his eyes.

Wynn dropped her head to his shoulder. "This is totally dumb, Zack. I'm more than capable of walking, you know."

"I know. But no one else seems to." He turned to Dani. "Stay right here with Josh, sweetheart."

"I will!"

Zack headed for the back door. Truth was, she felt good in his arms, a nice soft solid weight. Warm and very feminine. He liked holding her. And no way in hell was he going to let any of her "friends" pick her up so they'd experience the same sensations.

"They're just nettling you," Wynn said, "and you're

letting them." She reached down to open the kitchen door when Zack stopped in front of it.

"Where to?" he asked.

She sighed, then finally said, "The bathroom."

Zack grinned. The door closed behind them, shutting out some of the party noise. Now that they were in private, he nuzzled Wynn's ear, carefully because of his rough beard, and then asked, "Are you coming over tonight to...soak your foot?"

She looked up at him, surprised. "I thought you had plans?"

"I'll be free by eleven. It's been a total bitch of a day and I can't imagine a better way to end it than with a repeat of last night." He touched his mouth to hers and added, "That is, if you're up to it."

She said, "Ha! I sure wouldn't let a little broken toe keep me from it!"

Zack kissed her chin, feeling all his tension and aggravation melt away just from being near her. Leaving her behind this morning, knowing she was hurt, hadn't sat right with him. "And you called me a superhero," he teased gently.

Wynn hesitated, then made a face. "Okay, I give up. Just what are you doing tonight?"

They stood in the hallway outside the bathroom door. Wynn didn't ask to be put down, and Zack was in no hurry to release her. He looked at her mouth and wanted to groan. He could feel himself getting hard and ruthlessly brought himself under control.

"Del and Mick are coming over. They, Josh and I, are

going to watch an interview Del did for her upcoming book. It's going to be on channel—"

They heard a thump and looked up to see Conan collapsed against the wall, a large fist pressed to his massive chest.

Zack was briefly alarmed before Conan wheezed, "Delilah Piper is going to be here? Right next door? Oh my God."

"Delilah Piper-slash-Dawson. Remember, I told you Mick's funny about that. And yeah, she is."

Conan's eyes rolled back and he wheezed some more. "A celebrity in our midst! Wait until I tell everyone else."

"Conan," Wynn said suspiciously, "what are you doing in here?"

Briefly taken off guard, Conan stammered, then looked much struck. "I brought Ms. Piper's books over to be signed and I was going to give them to Zack!"

Wynn said, "Uh-huh."

"But now I can just give them to her myself." He rubbed his hands together. "I can't wait."

Whatever Conan had really wanted—and Zack assumed it was to check up on his sister—was forgotten as he rushed back outside to share the news.

Zack looked down at Wynn, then readjusted her weight so he could kiss her throat.

She sighed. "I'm sorry Zack, but I have a feeling your intimate little night with friends has just been ruined."

He kissed her throat again. "Conan is more than welcome. It'll tickle Del and it'll keep Mick on his toes. He gets rattled any time a guy looks at her with admiration—even if it's admiration for her work."

"Zack?"

"Hmmm?"

"You can set me down now."

"I'm not sure I want to."

Wynn hugged him, but said, "If you don't, Conan won't be the only one visiting us. My parents will come trooping through, too, and then the guys..."

Being especially careful of her injury, Zack slid her down his body. She kept her hands on his shoulders and her gaze on his mouth. "I like you in your uniform. It's sexy."

Zack grinned. "Is that right?"

She trailed her fingers over his jaw. "And this looks interesting, too."

"I didn't have time to shave this morning." He nuzzled her, letting her feel his whiskers. Then added in a gruff whisper, "But I'll shave before you come over tonight." He gazed down at her breasts and said, "I wouldn't want to give you a burn."

"Zack..."

The way she sighed his name was such a temptation. Zack turned her toward the bathroom. "Go, before I decide I can't wait until tonight."

She gave him a vacuous smile and hobbled in, favoring her injured foot while trying to strut like a man, just to prove she wasn't hurt. Zack shook his head and a warm feeling expanded inside him, making him hot and hard and filling him with tenderness.

Her ridiculous false bravado shouldn't have done that to him. *She* shouldn't have done that to him. But she did, and he knew he was in deep.

Problem was, for some strange reason, he just couldn't work up the energy to fight it.

10

IT WAS ELEVEN O'CLOCK and her parents had retired to their room half an hour ago. Wynn could still hear them talking and laughing, though. Because her parents remained frisky even after all these years, she made a mental note to run her ceiling fan at night for background noise, and slipped out of her room.

Unfortunately, she was almost to Zack's house when she realized the additional cars were still in his driveway; his company hadn't yet left. She was about to turn around when a female voice called out, "You must be Wynn."

Wynn froze. Zack had his porch light on and so did she, so she knew the woman could see her, but still she considered hiding.

The woman laughed. "I'm Del. Come on over and chat."

Wynn hadn't joined her brother and the others earlier when they'd gone to worship at the writer's feet. She wasn't much of a mystery reader, and beyond that, she hadn't liked the idea of forcing herself into Zack's company any more than she already had.

Her foot hurt and she was self-conscious in her robe,

but she crept forward and even pasted on a smile. "Hello. Yes, I'm Wynn. A neighbor."

Delilah Piper-Dawson stood leaning against a tree admiring the sky. When Wynn got close, Del offered her hand. "I've heard a lot about you."

"Oh?" Who had talked about her, she wondered. Zack? What had he said? She stepped closer.

Though Delilah was tall for a woman, Wynn towered over her. Del had the type of slender willowy build that made Wynn feel like a lumberjack.

Delilah looked her over and asked, "You're ready for bed?"

"Oh, no." She fidgeted with the belt to her terry cloth robe and explained, "I have my bathing suit on. Zack invited me to use his hot tub. I, uh, I broke my toe today."

"That's right! I heard about that, too."

Wynn studied the smaller woman. "What exactly has Zack told you?"

"Well, not much. Zack, as I'm sure you know, is very closemouthed and private."

Wynn didn't know any such thing.

"He's also very calm and controlled."

"Oh?"

Delilah laughed. "Yes, but Josh and Mick have both told me that around you, he's just the opposite. Always losing his temper and grumbling and growling. I love it. It was so funny when he first started talking about getting a wife. He had all these absurd notions of what qualities he'd want." Delilah shook her head and her beautiful, very shiny and sleek inky-black hair caught the moonlight, making it look almost liquid. Wynn reached up to smooth her own hair, which she'd ruthlessly contained in a tight knot on top of her head.

When she realized she was primping and why, Wynn dropped her hand and said again, "Oh?"

Delilah nodded. "Let me warn you though, if you do marry Zack, they'll all expect you to get dressed up for the wedding."

She said that as if it were the worst fate possible. Wynn despised dressing up, too, so she understood.

Del made a face. "But it's not that bad, considering the end results."

Wynn looked around, wondering what the hell she was supposed to say to that. When Delilah just waited, she blurted, "We won't be getting married. Zack isn't all that serious about me. He just wants to...well, he just *wants* me." And to be completely clear, she added, "But not for marriage."

Delilah stared at her, then took her arm. "Come on. Let's sit down. Here you are with a broken toe and I've got you standing in the yard sharing confidences." She turned, holding on to Wynn as if she, with her measly delicate strength, could offer substantial support. "Let's be really quiet though. The guys are yakking and I escaped out here to get some fresh air. I don't want them to join us yet."

They stopped at the hot tub and Delilah sat on the edge, crossing her ankles. "The patio curtains are closed," she pointed out, "so they won't notice us. You can go ahead and get in if you want."

Wynn shook her head.

"Okay, but let's get back to this sex business."

"I didn't exactly mean to say that." Wynn had no idea why she'd confessed such a thing to a complete stranger. Delilah had just asked and she'd answered.

"That's okay. People are always confiding in me. I'm a writer, you know."

Wynn had no idea what that had to do with anything.

"Your brother told me a lot about you, too. He says you've never been this serious about a guy before."

"I'll kill him."

Delilah laughed. "Don't worry. No one overheard him. But you should know, it's the same for Zack. I thought Mick was a recluse when it came to women, but Zack is even worse. It's amazing considering they're both friends with Josh, and that man knows no moderation where females are concerned."

Wynn started to say, "Oh?" but caught herself in time. "I gather Josh is something of a lady's man."

"He likes to think so. Unfortunately, most of the ladies agree with him." Then she said, "Now back to you and Zack. I want to tell you, whatever you do, don't give up. I almost gave up on Mick, but luckily his family talked me out of it. Since we're like Zack's family now, I feel honor bound to do the same for you."

Wynn gave up without a whimper. She flopped down beside Delilah on the edge of the tub and hung her head. "It's no wonder Zack isn't interested in getting serious with me. Every time I'm around him, I end up doing something dumb. Like wrestling him to the ground—"

"No kidding?" Delilah looked very curious about that.

"And insulting him and then I fell and broke my stupid toe..."

"Why do you insult him?"

Wynn shrugged. "I've always been treated like one of the guys. It's all I really know. I speak my mind, tease and harass."

Delilah nodded. "Yeah, Mick and Josh and Zack do that all the time."

"So does my brother and the guys from the gym."

"Hmmm." Delilah got up to pace. She wore a tiny T-shirt with a smiley face on the front, baggy jeans, and strappy sandals, and still she looked utterly feminine. If the woman wasn't being so nice, Wynn might not have liked her. She sat again and took Wynn's hand. "I think you should tell Zack how you feel."

"Really?" Wynn winced even considering it. "Is that what you did with Mick?"

She laughed. "Too much so. Poor Mick didn't know what to think of me. But I'm not used to hiding my feelings, especially feelings that strong. I knew almost from the moment I noticed him that I wanted him for my own."

Wynn nodded in understanding. She'd felt the same about Zack. Almost from the first, she'd known what a wonderful person he was.

"Okay." Delilah stood. "Off with the robe and into the hot tub. I'll get Mick and Josh to leave and I'll send Zack out. What's your bathing suit look like?" Her eyes widened and she asked with scandalized delight, "Or are you wearing one?"

"Of course I'm wearing one!" Wynn almost sputtered at the idea of traipsing across two yards in nothing but a thin robe. "I wouldn't leave my house naked."

Delilah looked let down. "Okay, let me see the suit."

"It's...um, kinda skimpy."

"Because you wanted to entice Zack? Good idea, not quite as good as being naked, but still... Not that he needs any enticement, you know. He's been antsy and pacing and impatient all night. We all knew he wanted us gone so he could visit with you, so of course that made Mick and Josh more determined to hang around, just to watch Zack fret." Delilah shook her head. "They're all nuts, but I love them."

Once she finished talking, Delilah just waited. Then she cleared her throat. "Can I see the suit?"

Wynn hadn't had any really close female friends before. She hung more with the guys, and that had always suited her just fine. But Delilah, well, she was easy to talk to, friendly and open. Wynn liked her on the spot.

"Okay, but don't laugh."

"Why would I laugh?"

Wynn squeezed her eyes shut, gripped the lapels of the robe, and held it open. She wasn't naked, but the string bikini was as close as she could get.

Delilah whistled. "Wow. Zack'll be lucky if he lasts half an hour. You look great. Like a model."

Wynn snatched the robe shut. "The only time Zack and I made love it was pitch dark and he couldn't really see me."

"Well, that suit'll make up for it! I almost wish I could hang around for his reaction. Will you call me tomorrow and let me know how it goes?"

Dumbstruck, Wynn stammered, "Uh, well, yeah. Sure."

"Wait! Better still, let's have lunch. I just finished a book so I've got some free time. I need to let my brain recoup before I start plotting again. Where do you work? I could meet you there."

Overwhelmed by Delilah's enthusiasm, Wynn heard herself giving the address for her brother's gym. "Conan will wet his pants if you actually come and say hi."

"Your brother is a real sweetheart. It always makes my day to meet up with a reader. In fact, don't tell him yet, but I'm thinking of setting a book around a gym. Can you imagine? With all that weight equipment and the pool and the sauna, why, all kinds of stuff could go on there. Like maybe..." Delilah caught herself and laughed. "There I go, plotting again. Ignore me."

Wynn was charmed. "I think it's interesting. And I'm sure Conan would be thrilled to help out by showing you around and answering questions." Her brother would owe her big time for this one, Wynn thought, and smiled.

"That'd be great. So what time is lunch?"

Delilah Piper-Dawson had a quick mind and Wynn could barely keep up. "Eleven-thirty?"

"Perfect. I'll be there. Now into the tub and I'll send Zack out."

"It was nice meeting you, Delilah."

Over her shoulder, Delilah said, "Same here. And call me Del."

Wynn stared after Delilah, feeling like she'd gotten seized in a whirlwind. Then she caught herself and realized Zack could be out any second. She didn't want to have to disrobe in front of him! She dropped the terry robe over a chair and slid into the warm water. The jets weren't turned on yet, but the hot water felt heavenly—and it covered her mostly bare body.

She only hoped Zack appreciated her immodesty.

ZACK STARED at Josh and Mick, who stared back, and wondered how in hell he could get rid of them. The show featuring Delilah's interview was long since over, but still they hung around, drinking more coffee and chatting as if no one had anywhere to go. Delilah had tired of it and gone outside to stretch her legs, or so she said.

No sooner did Zack think of her than she reappeared. She walked to her husband, took his hands and pulled him from the couch. "Let's go."

"Go where?" Mick asked, teasing her.

"Home. Zack has company and we've overstayed ourselves."

All three men turned to stare toward the kitchen where Del had entered. Zack asked, "Wynn is here?"

"No, her dad."

"*What?*"

Del laughed. "Just teasing. Yeah, it's Wynn. And what a nice woman! I really like her, Zack."

Zack's eyes narrowed. "Just how long has she been out there, Del?"

"About ten minutes, that's all." She winked. "We were chatting and getting to know each other."

Mick shook his head. "Honey, why didn't you bring her inside?"

"She didn't want to come in."

"Why not?"

"She's in this teeny tiny little string bikini."

With arrested looks on their faces, the men all turned toward the kitchen.

Del caught Mick around the neck. "Oh, no you don't. If you want to see a mostly naked woman, you can just take me on home."

Mick grinned and his dark eyes heated. "That's a hell of an idea."

Josh took two steps forward and Zack stepped in front of him. He crossed his arms. "I don't think so."

Trying for an innocent look, Josh said, "But it wouldn't be neighborly of me to leave without saying hello first."

"I'll give her your regrets and tell her you said 'hi.'"

Josh almost laughed. "Ah, c'mon, Zack. You can at least appease an old friend's curiosity."

"Get out. And you can leave by the front door."

Josh sauntered over to Del and slung an arm around her shoulder. "Del, honey, I guess you'll just have to tell me all about it."

Del smiled. "She's gorgeous, Josh. I can see why Zack is hooked." Then she turned to Zack. "But she's also very nice."

Josh nodded. "Agreed."

Zack hastily bent to kiss Del's cheek as she stepped out front. "Do me a favor, will you, hon? Make sure neither of them sneaks around back."

As soon as he got Del's laughing promise, Zack closed and locked his front door then raced for the patio. Dani was long since asleep, his company was finally gone, and Wynn was already in the tub. Finally, the day was beginning to improve.

He pushed the patio curtains aside and stared at Wynn for several seconds before opening the doors and stepping out. She looked beautiful, though he could only see her from the shoulders up. The rest of her was hidden beneath the water.

She had her impossible hair piled on top of her head, but the steam from the hot water had still affected it. Tiny curls at her temples sprang free, giving her the appearance of a newly hatched baby bird.

Zack smiled and he had to admit, it wasn't just lust making his stomach tight. "Hey."

Wynn lifted her head from the back of the tub and stared at him. "Hi."

Watching her, he began unbuttoning his shirt. "I

didn't realize you were here or I'd have come out sooner."

"That's okay. I didn't mean to interrupt your visit with your friends."

"Did you and Del have a nice chat?" More than anything, he wondered what they had talked about. With Del, there was no telling.

"She's really nice, isn't she?"

"Del's a sweetheart." He dropped his shirt and sat in a lawn chair to remove his shoes and socks. "Mick's crazy about her."

He set his shoes aside and stood to unfasten his slacks. He heard Wynn squeak, and looked up. "I'm not going to bother with trunks. You don't mind do you?"

She stared at his abdomen and shook her head. Zack was already so hard there was no way she could miss his erection. He wanted her, even more now that he'd had her and knew how incredible it was.

They were behind the privacy fence, so no one could see them. Still he reached inside and flipped off the lights, casting the hot tub into shadows.

Wynn muttered a complaint, which made him laugh. "Your eyes will adjust, but I don't want to take the chance of your parents wandering over."

"They're in bed," she said. "Nothing short of a natural disaster would get them out of there now."

Zack removed his wallet from his pocket. He took out two condoms and put them close at hand, then pulled his slacks and his boxers off and put them over the back of a chair. He stepped into the tub. "Do you want the jets, or is this good enough."

Wynn swallowed. He stood in front of her and he could feel her stare like a hot touch moving over his groin. He braced his legs apart and waited.

"Zack?"

"Yeah?"

"My eyes have adjusted."

He grinned and started to sit down, but she caught his hips. "No, wait just a minute. Let me...look. I didn't touch you much the other night. I kept thinking about that, you know, that I should have and wishing I had. Now I can."

Her hands slid down to his thighs then back up again. Zack watched her watching him, and it was so damned erotic he almost couldn't bear it. "I didn't give you much of a chance to touch me."

"You were remarkable." Without warning she leaned closer and cupped his testicles. Her hands were hot from being in the water, wet and gentle. His heart pounded.

She used her free hand to touch him everywhere, except where he most wanted her touch. His cock pulsed and flexed, but she ignored it as her wet palm moved over his lower back, his abdomen, his butt, with a gentle and exciting curiosity.

When she leaned forward and kissed his hipbone he groaned. "Wynn, you're a tease."

"No, I just want you so much. All of you."

Because she was always so open, so bold, he knew she meant it, every word.

He couldn't take it. He reached down, caught her wandering hand. "Right here, Wynn," he said, and curled her fingers around him.

Looking up at him, her beautiful eyes bright, she said, "Like this?"

A woman with large hands was a blessed thing, he decided. Her fingers circled him, firm but cautious, strong but soft. The contradictions made him wild. A sound of pleasure escaped his throat and he said, "Yeah."

Without releasing him, Wynn shifted to kneel in the tub. Zack caught sight of her barely contained breasts in the skimpy bikini top at the same time she indulged him with a long, slow, heated stroke.

Steam rose around him, expanded within him. He said, "That's enough," and reached for her hands.

"But..."

He hauled her up and held her in front of him. "Easy," he said, looking her over with hunger. "Don't hurt your foot."

She gave him a lopsided grin. "What foot?"

He smiled too, and reached out to cup her breast. "Christ, you're beautiful."

"I'm big," she said.

"And sexy."

"I've never worn a suit like this before."

"Thank God for small favors."

"My mother bought it for me when she was trying to get me married off."

His head snapped up. *"What?"*

Shrugging, Wynn explained, "I told you I don't date much. That bothers my folks. They hooked up young and they've always been happy and they want me happy."

Zack eased her closer, trying to quell the sick feeling in his stomach. "You need marriage to be happy?"

She looked away. "I'm in no hurry."

He wasn't at all sure he liked that answer anymore. "Why not?"

"Like you, I guess I'm looking for something special. That must be why I've never been that attracted to too many guys, right? And I did just get my own house. I want to have fun with it for a while before I start changing things again."

"I see." But he didn't, not really.

"Can we stop talking now?"

"You want to get on with it, do you?"

She moved her hands over his chest, and then lower. "Yes, I do."

Zack eased down into the water on the bench. "Come here, Wynn."

She stepped close and he reached around her to unhook her bikini bra. He draped it over the side of the tub. "One of these days," he said, "I'm going to get you laid out in the sunshine so I can see all of you." Before she could respond to that, he leaned forward and suckled her right nipple.

She clasped his head. "Zack!"

"Shh, sweetheart, keep it quiet. We don't want to wake anyone up."

He switched to her other breast, flicking her with his tongue, and she moaned low. "I'm ready now, Zack," she whispered urgently.

"Impossible," he said. "We're just getting started."

"But I've been thinking about it all day, even during that stupid party." She lifted his face to hers. "Please, Zack."

He stared at her while he slipped his fingers beneath the leg of her suit. Hot water swirled around her, but she was hotter still, wet and slick, her flesh swollen and soft. He removed his fingers and hastily pulled her bottoms off. Raising himself to the edge of the hot tub, he donned a condom, then eased back into the water to sit on the very edge of the bench seat.

"Straddle my hips, Wynn."

As she did so, her breasts moved over his chest, their skin wet and slippery and hot. He helped position her, taking care not to jostle her bruised foot.

"Brace your hands on my shoulders."

She did, and he eased up into her, hearing her soft moan, feeling the stretch of her inner muscles as she gripped him. He pressed his face into her throat, filled with so much emotion, so much pleasure, it was almost pain. He held her carefully and rather than thrust, he rocked them both, constantly kissing her and whispering to her; there was so much he wanted to say, but he didn't understand himself anymore. He only knew he wanted her, and now he had her.

When he felt Wynn tightening around him, he pressed his hand between their bodies and helped her along. She bit his shoulder as she came, and licked his mouth when he came seconds later.

Resting against him, she murmured, "Will we ever make love in a bed do you think?"

Zack wanted to say yes, that he wanted her in his bed right now. The more he saw her, the more he wanted to be with her. He didn't want to say good-night and send her back to her own home. He wanted to hold her all night, wake up with her in the morning, share breakfast with her and Dani, even argue with her.

But nothing was decided. All the issues still remained. He didn't have only himself to think about; he had to think of his daughter, too.

He said only, "I'm off for a week now. Dani has preschool two afternoons so the house will be free. If you can get away then..."

She kissed his chin. "I'll get away. But Zack?"

"Hmmm?" He'd just finished loving her, and already he was thinking of when he'd have her again. He felt obsessed.

"Are you seeing anyone else right now?"

"No, why?" He tried to see her face, but she kept it tucked close to his chest.

"You said you were looking for a wife. You said you had plans tomorrow night, too. I just wondered."

He smiled. "Tomorrow I planned to do my cleaning. That's all."

"Oh." She lifted up to look at him, winced when she bumped her toe, and finally got comfortable. "If you should decide to see anyone else, I want you to tell me."

Zack cupped her cheek, so smooth and sweet. "Why?"

"Because then I wouldn't see you anymore."

Just hearing her say it made him want to shout, made him want to drag her inside and keep her there. His chest felt tight, but he nodded. "All right." He smoothed his thumb over her bottom lip. "Same goes for me."

Wynn stared at him, then resettled herself on his chest. "All right."

11

"DO YOU TWO REALIZE we haven't been to Marco's in a month?"

Zack, sitting restlessly at his kitchen table, glanced up at Josh. Used to be he and Mick and Josh ate lunch at Marco's at least once a week. Now Mick was married and Zack...well, for the past three weeks he'd enjoyed spending his spare time with Wynn. She'd taken over his brain and his libido and probably even his heart.

That thought shook him and he stood to pace.

Mick chuckled. "There he goes again."

"Wynn has him on the run." Josh laughed. "Not that it'll do him any good. You were as bad once."

Mick just shrugged. "It's scary falling in love."

Feeling haunted, Zack turned to scowl at them. Love? *Love.* He hadn't known her long enough, only a little over a month, but he did know she wasn't what he'd always wanted in a female. She obviously had what he enjoyed, but that kind of enjoyment wasn't appropriate for the father of a little girl.

He said very quietly, "Shit."

"Oh give it up, Zack." Josh threw a potato chip at him and it bounced off his chest. "You walk around looking like a dying man, and there's no reason for it. Just bite the bullet. Tell her how you feel."

Even now, Dani was next door with Wynn. They were sitting in the grass, a giant roll of paper between them, finger painting. It had become Dani's favorite new pastime, thanks to Chastity. She and Artemus, with all their outrageous, oddball, delightful ways, had become surrogate grandparents and his daughter loved them. They hadn't yet found a place of their own, but Zack knew when they did move, Dani would miss them.

It was nearing Halloween and the fall air had cooled, breezing in through the open kitchen window and the screen door. But still Zack felt too hot, too contained. He dropped back into his chair and said, "I don't know."

Mick sipped his coffee. "Don't know what?"

"Anything. I don't know what to do, what I feel."

Josh offered, "She's a pretty special woman."

Zack propped his head on his open palms and tunneled his fingers through his hair. "She's not what I was looking for."

"I wasn't looking for anyone when I found Delilah. It doesn't make any difference."

"I can't just think about myself."

Josh tipped his head. "What the hell does that mean?"

"It means I'm a father. I have to consider Dani."

"Dani adores her, and vice versa."

Zack clenched his hair. "I wanted someone domestic, someone calm and reasonable."

Josh laughed out loud. "Domestic you got. Calm and reasonable? And you wanted her to be female right? Good luck."

"Having women troubles, Josh?" Zack asked suspiciously.

Mick grinned. "Woman—singular. Amanda Barker, the lady putting together the charity calendar? Well, they've already started shooting and Josh here still hasn't agreed. She's getting…insistent. Seems she won't take no for an answer."

"She's a pain in the ass." Josh shrugged. "Everywhere I turn, there she is. But I just ignore her."

Zack dropped his hands and shook his head. "Yeah, right. Like you'd ignore any woman."

Josh sat back and crossed his arms behind his head, a man at his leisure. "She's not like Del and Wynn."

Both Mick and Zack straightened. "What are you talking about?"

"They're real women, straightforward, funny, down to earth. They don't whine and cry and complain just to get their way, and they don't continually fuss with their nails and their hair. I doubt you'd catch either of them getting a facial. I like all that earthiness." He nudged Mick with his elbow and said, "They're both everything a guy could want—and more."

Mick glanced at Zack. "Do you want to kill him or should I?"

Zack shook his head. Everything Josh claimed was true. Wynn worked hard, played and laughed hard, and she never seemed concerned with the typical things women considered. Not in a million years could he imagine her whining. "I think your Amanda sounds responsible."

"She's not *my* Amanda, and yeah, so? Wynn is responsible."

Zack stood again. "Ha! Wynn is outrageous. She speaks before she thinks, acts before she's considered the consequences. She pretends to be one of the guys and dresses so damn sexy it makes me nuts."

Mick and Josh looked at each other. "She wears sloppy clothes."

"Sloppy sexy clothes that fit her body and show glimpses of skin and... How the hell would I live with someone like that?"

Mick stared down at his coffee mug. Very quietly, he asked, "How would you live without her?"

Zack drew back. Feeling desperate, he said, "Dani has all of us to teach her to do guy things. I wanted a woman who would be a good influence on her, someone who did all those female things you just mentioned, Josh. Someone to be a role model, ya know?"

"You're an ass, Zack." Josh shook his head in pity. "Wynn is terrific. She's independent and intelligent and honest. Yeah she's outspoken, but so what? You never have to guess at what she's thinking. And I like the way she dresses."

Zack's eyes nearly crossed. Josh had totally missed the point. He opened his mouth to explode with frustration, and noticed Wynn standing frozen just outside the open kitchen door. "Oh, hell."

Without a word, Wynn jerked around and hurried away. Zack took off after her, slamming the screen door open in his haste. Before it could slam closed again, Josh and Mick were on his heels.

"Wynn!"

"Go to hell!" she shouted over her shoulder. She all but ran—*from him*—on her not yet healed foot and Zack worried. The blasted woman hadn't even given him a chance to explain!

He stomped after her, cursing her impetuous reaction, worrying about her foot because he knew *she* wouldn't worry about it. Her legs were long and strong, but his were as long, and whether she wanted to believe it or not, stronger. He closed the distance between them.

From Wynn's yard, he saw his daughter and Chastity look up. On the patio, Artemus and Conan, along with Marc and Clint and Bo all lifted their heads. He could hear Mick and Josh just behind him.

His jaw clenched. When he got hold of Wynn, he thought he might strangle her.

He reached out, caught her arm—and she whipped around on him in a fury, letting out a war cry that rattled his ears and totally took him by surprise. She jerked his arm, stuck her foot out and sent him sprawling.

For three seconds Zack lay flat on his back, staring up at the blue sky, hearing snickers and whispers and feeling his temper rise.

Wynn leaned over him, her eyes red and her mouth pinched. "Don't ever touch me again. You want rid of me, well you're rid of me!"

In a flash, he grabbed her elbow and tossed her to her back beside him.

She yelled, "My foot!" and Zack froze at the thought of hurting her.

At the same moment he heard Conan call out, "It's a trick!" but it was too late.

Wynn landed on top of him, her knees on his shoulders, her hands pinning his wrists to the ground, her big behind on his diaphragm. He could barely breathe. "For the record, you miserable jerk, I never asked to be your wife. As to that, I wouldn't be your wife now if you went down on your knees."

It was hard, but Zack managed not to laugh. The fact that he couldn't draw a deep breath with her bouncing astride him helped. "You were eavesdropping!"

"Another of my less than sterling qualities," she sneered. "But don't worry." She leaned in, almost smothering him with her breasts—not that he was complaining. "I won't force myself on you anymore. You're free to go find your little paragon of domesticity! I wish you luck."

She started to rise, still a little awkwardly since her toe hadn't entirely healed, and Zack caught her with his legs. "Oh, no you don't!" He flipped her again and sprawled his entire weight on top of her. He heard her loud grunt, but paid no mind. "You don't get to just barge in in a huff after listening to a private conversation, just to give me hell and then leave."

Wynn bowed and jerked and, realizing she couldn't throw him off, she subsided. "I get to do whatever I please! It's none of your damn business." She looked him over with disdain, but Zack saw her bottom lip tremble. "Not anymore."

His heart hurt. Emotion swelled inside him. "Wynn."

She jerked again, but couldn't free herself. "I don't even know why I bothered with you," she muttered.

He wanted to kiss her, but figured if he loosened his grip at all, she'd run from him again. "Because I'm sweet?"

"Ha!"

"You're the one who said it, Wynn, not me."

He heard low voices and looked up to see everyone gathered around them wearing expressions of curiosity and expectation and anticipation. They blocked the sun.

He turned back to Wynn. "You're not walking out on me."

"I don't think she was walking," Bo pointed out. "Looked more like running."

"Did to me, too," Josh agreed. "Not that I blame her."

To hell with it, Zack thought, and he leaned down to kiss her. She almost bit him, but he laughed and pulled away. She looked ready to spit on him, and he said, "I love you, Wynn."

Her gorgeous golden eyes widened, and then they both *oofed* when Dani leaped onto Zack's back and began hopping up and down. "We're keeping her, we're keeping her!"

Laughing, Zack said, "Not yet, honey. She has to tell me she loves me, too."

Dani flattened herself on Zack's back and leaned over

his shoulder into Wynn's frozen face. She put her tiny hand on Wynn's cheek and said, "I want you for my mommy."

Wynn drew a broken, shuddering breath and said, "Ohhh," and her face crumbled. She blinked hard, but big tears welled up.

Zack turned his head to kiss his daughter's cheek. "Move, Dani."

"'Kay, Dad." She scampered off and stood there fretting until Mick picked her up and whispered something in her ear. Then she smiled and nodded.

Zack nudged Wynn with his nose. "We need privacy, sweetheart. Don't fight me, okay?"

She nodded, attempting to duck her face against him. Knowing Wynn as well as he did, Zack imagined that to her, a spate of tears equaled the gravest humiliation. She would laugh heartily, yell like a fishmonger, and she loved him with enough intensity to leave him insensate. But she wanted to hide her upset.

He'd allow her to hide her tears from the others, but he didn't want her hiding anything from him.

Zack stood, hauled Wynn over his shoulder and turned away from everyone to head back into the privacy of his house.

Conan yelled, "For once in your life, Wynonna, be reasonable! Don't blow it."

Bo and Clint and Marc all laughed, offering suggestions to Zack on how to best her. They said, "Watch her legs!" and "She fights dirty, so protect yourself," and

"If she gets the upper hand, just remember that she's ticklish!"

Zack waved his free hand in an absent "thank you."

Artemus called out, "Darling, I *will* do something with your hair for the wedding, so get used to the idea right now!"

At that dire threat, Wynn started to push up, but Zack put his hand on her bottom to hold her still. Grinning like a fool, he realized he felt better than good. He felt...incredible.

He went through the kitchen and the living room, took the stairs two at a time, went into his room and dumped Wynn on his bed. He rubbed his back and groaned dramatically. "Damn, you're heavy."

She held her arms out to him.

Amazing, Zack thought, loving the sight of her in his bed and knowing he wanted to see her there every day for the rest of his life. He lowered himself onto her. "I love you," he said again.

She squeezed him tight. "I love you, too."

His heart expanded until it nearly choked him. "Enough to marry me and be Dani's mommy?"

She pushed him away. "I won't change for you, Zack." Her eyes glistened with tears, but she still looked ferocious. "I am who I am, and I like me."

"I like you, too." He kissed the end of her nose and smiled. "You scare me to death, sometimes infuriate me and drive me to unheard of depths of jealousy, but I wouldn't want you to change, sweetheart. Well, except that I'm going to have to insist all other males keep their hands off you. Other than that..."

She laughed and swatted him, but her humor ended with a quiver. "I so badly wanted to be Dani's mommy. I love her so much." More tears gathered in her eyes and she groaned. "Oh God, this is awful." She used his shoulder to wipe her eyes.

Zack smiled. She so seldom said the expected. "How would you feel about giving Dani a brother? She mentioned that, too."

"She did?"

"Yes. Back when she first explained to me that she was going to keep you."

Wynn drew a shaky breath. "I'm twenty-eight. I'd like to have a baby before I'm thirty."

"In other words, you want me to get right on it?" He nudged her again. "I'm ready, willing and able. And I love you."

She choked back a sob and then viciously shook her head. "Josh would be appalled if he saw me snuffling like an idiot."

Zack kissed her wet cheeks and then the corner of her mouth. "Who cares what Josh thinks?"

"I care what Josh thinks. After all, he's the one who changed your mind about me."

Zack laughed. "I already knew I loved you and you can believe Josh didn't have a damn thing to do with it."

"Right. So what was all that in the kitchen about?"

He shrugged. "I was just mouthing off, fighting the

inevitable, posturing like any respectable man would do." He eyed her and said, "*You* ought to understand that."

She made a face. "I heard you, Zack. I'm not at all who you wanted."

"But you're who I love. You're who I need." He cupped her face and kissed her. "Ever since meeting you, I've been thinking about leaving the field, becoming an instructor. I even took steps in that direction."

"You have?"

"And I've thought about moving Dani's room farther down the hall to the guest room—something she's mentioned before because that room's bigger, but I always wanted her close and until you, I never considered having a woman in the house with Dani. Then I started thinking about privacy."

Her brows lowered in thought. "You do get rather loud when you're excited," she remarked with grave seriousness. "You groan and if I touch you right here, you shout and—"

Zack drew away her teasing hand and quieted her with a mushy, laughing kiss. "Wynn, I know you won't be easy to control—"

"Control!" She reached for him again and he pinned her down.

"—but the upside to that is we'll get to spend lots of time wrestling." He bobbed his eyebrows. "And now that I've made up my mind, you should know I'm not at all sweet. I'm actually ruthless when there's something—or someone—I want."

Wynn quit struggling and gave him a coy look. "And you want me?" He pushed against her, letting her feel his erection. She grinned. "Well, since we love each other, then I suppose we should get married."

Zack collapsed on her. "Thank God. You do know how to drag out the suspense, don't you?"

"There's something you should know, though."

He opened one eye.

"My parents have already told me that if we marry, they want my house." Zack made a strangled sound, but she quickly continued. "I think they suspected this might happen, which is why they let you carry me off and why they've only been halfheartedly looking for another place to stay." She pressed back so she could see his face, and with a crooked impish grin, added, "But I know how you feel about awkwardness with neighbors..."

He pinched her for that bit of impertinence, then grunted when she pinched him back.

Zack rolled so that she was atop him. "I like your folks and so does Dani. As long as you live with me, the rest doesn't matter." They kissed and it was long minutes later before Zack again lifted his head and looked down the long length of his future wife. "We're going to need a bigger bed."

Wynn immediately asked, "Do you think Dani would like to be a flower girl?"

Zack laughed. "At least it'd get her into a dress."

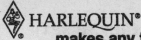

Celebrate the season with

Midnight Clear

**A holiday anthology featuring
a classic Christmas story from
New York Times bestselling author**

Debbie Macomber

**Plus a brand-new *Morgan's Mercenaries* story
from *USA Today* bestselling author**

Lindsay McKenna

**And a brand-new *Twins on the Doorstep* story
from national bestselling author**

Stella Bagwell

Available at your favorite retail outlets in November 2001!

Silhouette®

Where love comes alive™

Visit Silhouette at www.eHarlequin.com

PSMC

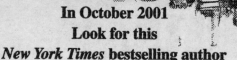
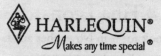

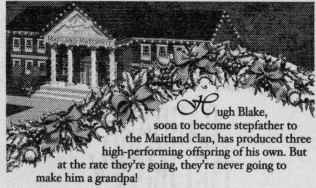

Hugh Blake, soon to become stepfather to the Maitland clan, has produced three high-performing offspring of his own. But at the rate they're going, they're never going to make him a grandpa!

There's *Suzanne*, a work-obsessed CEO whose Christmas spirit could use a little topping up....

And *Thomas*, a lawyer whose ability to hold on to the woman he loves is evaporating by the minute....

And *Diane*, a teacher so dedicated to her teenage students she hasn't noticed she's put her own life on hold.

But there's a Christmas wake-up call in store for the Blake siblings. Love *and* Christmas miracles are in store for all three!

Maitland Maternity Christmas

A collection from three of Harlequin's favorite authors

Muriel Jensen
Judy Christenberry
& Tina Leonard

Look for it in November 2001.